she was trembling with the agility of new spring buds in the wind then it was because of her shock.

If she felt weak, and her heart was pounding with dangerous speed, then it was because of the weight of her gown. If she couldn't move then it was because of the arms that imprisoned her.

It was because her heart was racing so fast that his own had started to pound heavily, Max told himself. It was because the walls either side of the steps enclosed them that he was so conscious of the scent of her hair and her skin. It was because he was a man and she was a woman that his body was flooded with an unwanted surge of physical arousal that had him tightening his hold on her.

Extreme danger and extreme desire went hand in hand, and produced between them an extreme pleasure that was an almost unbearable delight. A delight that was merely a foretaste of what the night that lay before them would hold.

Penny Jordan has been writing for more than twenty years and has an outstanding record: over 170 novels published, including the phenomenally successful A PERFECT FAMILY, TO LOVE, HONOUR AND BETRAY, THE PERFECT SINNER and POWER PLAY, which hit the *Sunday Times* and *New York Times* bestseller lists. Penny Jordan was born in Preston, Lancashire, and now lives in rural Cheshire.

Recent titles by the same author:

THE SICILIAN BOSS'S MISTRESS*
THE SICILIAN'S BABY BARGAIN*
CAPTIVE AT THE SICILIAN BILLIONAIRE'S
   COMMAND*
TAKEN BY THE SHEIKH
THE SHEIKH'S BLACKMAILED MISTRESS
VIRGIN FOR THE BILLIONAIRE'S TAKING

The Leopardi Brothers

A BRIDE FOR HIS MAJESTY'S PLEASURE

BY
PENNY JORDAN

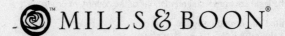

All the characters in this book have no existence outside the imagination of the author, and have no relation whatsoever to anyone bearing the same name or names. They are not even distantly inspired by any individual known or unknown to the author, and all the incidents are pure invention.

HOUNSLOW LIBRARIES

ISL

C0000 002 471 894

HJ	16-Oct-2009
AF ROM	£3.19

First published in Great Britain 2009
Harlequin Mills & Boon Limited,
Eton House, 18-24 Paradise Road, Richmond, Surrey TW9 1SR

© Penny Jordan 2009

ISBN: 978 0 263 87443 3

Set in Times Roman 10½ on 12¼ pt
01-1109-47107

Harlequin Mills & Boon policy is to use papers that are natural, renewable and recyclable products and made from wood grown in sustainable forests. The logging and manufacturing process conform to the legal environmental regulations of the country of origin.

Printed and bound in Spain
by Litografia Rosés, S.A., Barcelona

A BRIDE FOR
HIS MAJESTY'S
PLEASURE

PROLOGUE

'AND if I refuse to marry you?' Although she did her best not to allow her feelings to show, she was conscious of the fact that her voice trembled slightly.

Max looked at her.

'I think you already know the answer to your own question.'

The dying sun streaming in through the tower window warmed the darkness of her hair and revealed the classical beauty of her facial bone structure, before stroking golden fingers along the exposed column of her throat.

A twenty-first-century woman, caught in an ancient and powerful trap of savagery and custom, Max acknowledged wryly, if only to himself.

The intensity of the powerful and unwanted emotional and physical reaction that punched through him caught him off guard. It was a dangerous mix of sympathy and desire, neither of which he should be feeling. But most especially not the desire. Immediately Max turned away from her—like a schoolboy desperate to conceal the over-enthusiastic and inappropriate reaction of his developing maleness, he derided himself.

But he was not a schoolboy, and furthermore he was perfectly capable of controlling both his emotions and his physical desire. So his own body had momentarily caught him off guard? It would not happen again.

What he was doing wasn't something he wanted to do, nor was it in any way for his own benefit. It was a duty, and she was the doorway via which he could access what he needed to help those who needed it so desperately. It was a loathsome situation; either he sacrificed her, and in a sense himself, or he risked sacrificing his people. He did not have the luxury of indulging in personal and private emotional needs. His duty now obliged him to channel his thoughts and feelings towards those to whom he had given his commitment when he had accepted the crown and become the ruling Prince of Fortenegro. His people. This woman's people.

He turned back towards her. So much was at stake; the future of a whole country lay in this woman's hands. He would have preferred to be honest with her—but how could he, given her family background? She was a rich man's grandchild. Her grandfather a man, he knew now, who had alternated between both over-indulging his grandchildren and over-controlling them—to the extent that they had become adept at deceit and were motivated only by self interest.

Ionanthe looked at the man facing her—a man who represented so much that she hated.

'You mean that I'll be thrown to the wolves, so to speak? In the form of the people? Forced to pay my family's debt of honour to you?'

When he gave no reply she laughed bitterly.

'And you dare to call yourself civilized?'

'I own neither the crime nor its punishment. I am as impotent in this situation as you are yourself,' Max defended himself caustically.

Impotent. It was a deliberately telling choice of word, surely, given that he had just told her that she must marry him and give him a son as recompense for her sister's crimes against him. Or be handed over to the people to be tried by a feudal form of justice that was no justice at all.

As he waited for her response Max thought back over the events that had led them both to this unwanted impasse.

CHAPTER ONE

'THERE must be vengeance, Highness.' The courtier was emphatic and determined as he addressed Max.

The Count no doubt considered him ill fitted for his role of ruler of the island of Fortenegro—the black fort, so named originally because of the sheer dark cliffs that protected the mainland facing side of the island.

'Justice must be seen to be done,' Count Petronius continued forcefully.

The Count, like most of the courtiers, was in his late sixties. Fortenegro's society was fiercely patriarchal, and its laws harsh and even cruel, reflecting its refusal to move with the times. A refusal which Max fully intended to change. The only reason he had not flatly refused to step into his late cousin's shoes and become the new ruler of the principality was because of his determination to do what he knew his late father had longed to do—and that was to bring Fortenegro, and more importantly its people, out of the Dark Ages and into the light of the twenty-first century. That, though, was going to take time and patience, and first he must win the respect of his people and, just as importantly, their trust.

Fortenegrans were constitutionally opposed to change—especially, according to his courtiers, any kind of change that threatened their way of life and the beliefs that went with that way of life: beliefs such as the need to take revenge for insults and slights both real and imagined.

'An eye for an eye; a tooth for a tooth—that is the law of our people,' the Count continued enthusiastically. 'And they will expect you to uphold it. In their eyes a prince and a ruler who cannot protect his own honour cannot be trusted to protect theirs. That is their way and the way they live.'

And not just them, Max reflected grimly as he looked one by one at the group of elderly courtiers who had been his late cousin's advisers and who, in many ways, despite the fact that he was now ruler of the island, were still reluctant to cede to him the power they had taken for themselves during his late cousin's reign. But then Cosmo had been a playboy, unashamedly hedonistic and not in the least bit interested in the island he ruled or its people—only the wealth with which it had provided him.

Cosmo, though, was dead—dying at thirty-two of the damage inflicted by the so-called 'recreational' drugs to which he had become addicted. He'd been without a son to succeed him, leaving the title to pass to Max.

Justice must indeed be seen to be done, Max knew, but it would be *his* justice, not theirs, done in his way and according to his judgement and his beliefs.

The most senior of his late cousin's advisers was speaking again.

'The people will expect you to revenge yourself on the family of your late wife because of her betrayal of you.'

Max knew that the Count and Eloise's grandfather had been sworn enemies, united only by their shared adherence to a moral code that was primitive and arcane. Now, with Eloise and her grandfather dead, he was being urged to take revenge on the sole remaining member of the family—his late wife's sister—for Eloise's betrayal of their marriage and her failure to provide him with the promised heir.

In the eyes of his people it was not merely his right but his duty to them as their ruler to carry out full vengeance according to the ancient laws relating to any damage done to a man's honour. His late wife's family must make full restitution for the shame she had brought on them and on him. Traditionally, that meant that the dishonoured husband could set aside the wife who had betrayed him and take in her place one of her sisters or cousins, who must then provide him with the son his wife's betrayal had denied him.

These were ancient laws, passed down by word of mouth, and Max was appalled at the thought of giving in to them and to those who clung so fiercely to them. But he had no choice. Not if he wanted to win the trust of his people. Without that trust he knew that he could not hope to change things, to bring the island and those who lived there into the modern world. He had already sacrificed his personal beliefs once by marrying Eloise in the first place. Did he really want to do so a second time? Especially when it meant involving someone else? And if so, why?

The status and wealth of being the island's ruler meant little to him. He was already wealthy, and the very idea of one person 'ruling' others went against his strongest beliefs.

But he *was* the island's ruler, whether he wanted to be or not, and as such he owed its people—his people—a duty of care. He might never succeed in bringing change to the older generation, but for the sake of their children and their children's children he had to win the trust of the leaders and the elders so that those changes could be slowly put in place.

Refusing to accept their way of life and ignoring the laws that meant so much to them would only create hostility. Max knew all these things, but still the whole idea of honour and vengeance was repugnant to him.

A year ago he would have laughed in disbelief at the very idea that he might find himself the ruler of an island in the Aegean off the coast of Croatia.

He had known about the island and its history, of course. His father had spoken often of it, and the older brother with whom he had quarrelled as a young man—because his brother had refused to acknowledge that for the sake of the island's people it was necessary to spend some of his vast fortune on improving the quality of their lives and their education.

Max's father had explained to him that the island was locked in its own past, and that the men who had advised his grandfather and then his own father were hostile to modernisation, fearing for their wealth and status.

His father, with his astute brain and compassion for the human race, had proved that being wealthy and being a philanthropist were far from mutually exclusive, and after the death of his parents Max had continued with their charitable work as head of the foundation his father had started. Under Max's financial guidance both his own personal wealth and that of the foundation had grown, and Max had joined the exclusive ranks of that small and discreet group of billionaires who used their wealth for the benefit of others. Anonymity was a prized virtue of this group of generous benefactors. Max was as different from his late cousin as it was possible to be.

Physically, Max had inherited through his father's genes the tall, broad-shouldered physique of the warrior princes who had coveted and conquered the island many generations ago, along with thick dark hair and a profile that could sometimes look as though it had been hewn from the rock that protected the island from its enemies, so little did his expression give away.

Only his slate-blue eyes came from his English mother; the rest of him was, as his father had often said, 'pure Fortenegro and its royal house.' The evidence of the truth of that statement could be seen in the profile stamped into the island's ancient coinage, but whilst outwardly he might resemble his ancestors, inwardly Max was his own man—a man who fully intended to remove from the people of the island the heavy yoke of custom and oppression under which they lived.

When he had first come to the island to take up the reins of ruling he had promised himself that he would bring the people out of the darkness of poverty and lack of opportunity into the light. But it was proving a far harder task than he had anticipated.

The men who formed his 'court', instead of supporting him, were completely antagonistic towards any kind of modernisation, and continually warned him of the risk of riots and worse from the people if their way of life were to be challenged.

In an attempt to do the right thing Max had married the granddaughter of one of his nobles—a marriage of mutual convenience, which Eloise had assured him she wanted, saying that she would be proud to provide the island with its next ruler. What she had not told him was that whilst she was happy to become his Princess, she had no intention of giving up her regular pasttime of taking a lover whenever she felt like it—foreigners, normally, who had come to the island for one reason or another.

Within hours of the deaths of Eloise and her current lover, when their car had plunged over one of Fortenegro's steep cliffs, gossip about her relationship with the man she had been with had begun. A maid at the castle had seen Eloise in bed in her grandfather's apartment with her lover, and before too long the whole island had known.

Now, six months after her death and following the death of her grandfather, his barons were pressing him to exact revenge on her family for her betrayal.

'It is your duty,' his courtiers had insisted. 'Your late wife's sister must make restitution. She must provide you with the son your wife denied you. That is the way of our people. Your wife shamed you. Only by taking her sister can that shame be expunged and both your honour and the honour of her family be restored.'

'I doubt that Eloise's sister would agree with you.'

Neither his wife nor her grandfather had ever spoken much about Eloise's sister. All Max knew about her, other than the fact that she existed, was that, having trained as an economist, she now lived and worked in Europe.

'She no longer lives here,' Max had pointed out. 'And if she is as intelligent as she seems she will not return, knowing what awaits her.'

'She is already on her way back,' Max had been told by Count Petronius, who had continued smoothly, 'I have taken it upon myself to summon her on your behalf.'

Max had been furious.

'So that she can be threatened into paying her family's supposed debt of honour?' he had demanded angrily.

The Count had shrugged his shoulders. 'I have told her that the apartment in the palace occupied by her late grandfather must be cleared of his possessions. Since he occupied the apartment for many years she will naturally wish to remove from it those things that may be of value.'

Max hadn't been able to conceal his loathing for the Count's underhanded behaviour.

'You have tricked and trapped her.'

'It is your own fate you should be considering, not hers,' the Count had pointed out. 'The people will not tolerate being shamed by a ruler who allows his wife to cuckold him. They will expect you to demand a blood payment.'

And if I do not? Max had wanted to demand. But he had known the answer.

'We live in troubled times,' the Count had told him. 'There are those on the mainland who look at this island and covet it for their own reasons. If the islanders were to rise up against you because they felt you had let them down then such people would be pleased. They would be quick to seize the advantage you will have given them.'

Max had frowned. The Count might have spoken theatrically, but Max knew that there was indeed a cadre of very very rich and unscrupulous businessmen who would like very much indeed to take over the island and use it for their own purposes. The island was rich in minerals, and it would be a perfect tax haven. And so much more than that. With its natural scenic beauty— its snow in winter on the high ridge of its mountains, and its sea facing beaches that basked in summer sunshine—it would make a perfect tourist destination, providing year-round enjoyment.

Max was already aware of the benefits that tourism could bring to the people of the island—handled properly—but he was equally aware of the billions it could make for the unscrupulous, and the destruction and damage they would cause if they were allowed to gain control of the island. He had a duty to ensure that did not happen.

'Your late wife's sister is on her way here, and once she is here you must show the people the power of your vengeance. Only then will you have their respect and their trust,' the Count had continued.

And now he must wait for the woman standing opposite him to give him her answer—and he must hope, for her sake and the sake of his people, that she gave him the right one, even whilst he abhorred the way she had been tricked into coming to the island, and the nature of the threats against her personal safety.

If nothing else, he told himself grimly, when she married him he would at least be able to protect her from the appalling situation the Count had outlined to him— even if that protection did come at the cost of her personal freedom.

Certain aspects of his current position were never going to sit comfortably with his personal moral code, Max acknowledged grimly. It was all very well for him. He was making the decision to sacrifice his freedom of choice for the sake of his people. Ionanthe did not have that choice. She was being *forced* to sacrifice hers.

CHAPTER TWO

THE sun was sinking swiftly into the Aegean sea whilst the man who had been her sister's husband—who now wanted her to take Eloise's place—stood in silence by the window. The evening breeze ruffled the thick darkness of his hair. With that carved, hawkish over-proud profile he could easily have belonged to another age. He *did* belong to another age—one that should no longer be allowed to exist. An age in which some men were born to grind others beneath their heels and impose their will on them without mercy or restraint.

Well, she wasn't going to give in—no matter how much he threatened her. She had been a fool to let herself be tricked into coming here, especially when she knew what the old guard of the island were like. That was why she had left in the first place. Was it really only a handful of hours ago that she had been promising herself that finally, with her grandfather's death and the money she would inherit, she would be free to do what she had wanted to do for so long. Offer her services as an economist to what she considered to be the most

forward-thinking and socially responsible charitable organisation in the world—The Veritas Foundation.

Ionanthe had first heard about Veritas when she had
been working in Brussels. A male colleague to whom she
had taken a dislike had complained about the charity,
saying that its aims of alleviating poverty and oppression
by offering education and the hope of democracy to the
oppressed was just a crazy idealist fantasy. Ionanthe had
been curious enough about the organisation to want to
find out more, and what she had learned had filled her
with an ambition to one day be part of the dedicated
team of professionals who worked for the charity. The
Foundation was about doing things for others, not self-
aggrandisement, and she approved of that as much as she
did *not* approve of her homeland's new ruler.

As far as she was concerned, the island's new Prince
was every bit as bad as those who had gone before him.
He expected her to take Eloise's place and wipe out the
shame staining both his reputation and that of her
family—to give him the son Eloise had not. A son who
would one day rule in his place.

A son, an heir. A future ruler.

All of a sudden a sense of prescient awareness so
powerful that it reached deep down into the most secret
places of her heart shuddered through her, warning her that
she stood at a crossroads that would affect not just her own
life but more importantly the lives of others—not for one
generation, but for the whole future of her people.

She might originally have studied law and gone to
Brussels hoping to make changes that would benefit
the lives of others, but she had gradually become disil-

lusioned and the bright hopes of her dreams had become tarnished. Now she could do something for others—something just as important in its way as the work she might have been able to do via the Veritas Foundation.

The man confronting her needed an heir. A son. *Her* son. A son born of her who, with her love and guidance, would surely become a ruler who would be everything a good ruler should be—a ruler who would honour and love his people, who would guide them to a better future, who would understand the importance of providing them with proper education. A ruler who would build hospitals and schools, who would give his people pride in themselves and their future instead of tethering them to the past.

Hope and determination gathered force inside her like a tidal wave, surging up from the depths of her being, refusing to allow anything to stand in its way. Her breath caught in her throat, lifting her breasts. The movement caught Max's attention. His late wife had considered herself to be a beauty, a *femme fatale* whom no man could resist, but her sister had a darker, deeper female magic that owed nothing to the expensive beauty treatments and designer clothes Eloise had loved. The promise of true sensuality surrounded her like an invisible aura. Max frowned. The last thing he wanted was another wife whose sex drive might take her into the arms and the beds of other men. But against his will, against logic and wisdom, he could feel the magnetic pull of her sensuality on his own senses.

He dismissed the warning note being struck within him—he had been too long without a woman. But, since he was thirty-four years old, and not twenty-four, he was perfectly capable of subsuming his sexual desire and channelling his energies into other less dangerous responses.

Unexpectedly, irrationally and surely foolishly a small thrill of excitement surged through Ionanthe. She had the power to give Fortenegro a prince—a leader who would truly lead its people to freedom.

She looked at Max. He exuded power and confidence. His features were strongly drawn into lines of raw masculinity, his cheekbones and jaw carved and sculpted and then clothed in flesh in a way that drew the female eye. Yes, he was very good-looking—if one liked that particular brand of hard-edged arrogant male sexuality and darkly brooding looks. He carried within his genes the history of all those who had ruled Fortenegro: Moorish warriors, Crusaders, Norman knights, and long before them Egyptians, Phoenicians, Greeks and Romans. He wore his pride like an invisible cloak that swung from his shoulders as surely as a real one had swung from the shoulders of those who had come here and stamped their will on the island—just as he was now trying to stamp his will on her.

But she had her own power—the power of giving the island a ruler who would truly be an honourable man and a wise and just prince—her son by this man who had brought her here to be a flesh-and-blood sacrifice— a destiny that belonged in reality to another age. But she was a woman of this modern age, a twenty-first-century woman with strong beliefs and values. She was no helpless victim but a woman with the strength of mind and of purpose to shape events to match her own goals.

She was no young, foolish girl with a head and a heart filled with silly dreams. Yes, once she had yearned to find love, a man who would share her crusading need to right the wrongs of the past and to work for the good of her people. She had known that she would never find him on the island, governed by men like her grandfather, who adhered to the old ways, but she had not found him in Brussels either, where she had quickly learned that a sincere smile could easily mask a liar and a cheat. Powerful men had desired her—powerful married men. She had refused them, whilst the men she *had* accepted had ultimately turned out to be weak and incapable of matching her hunger for equality and justice for those denied those things. She was twenty-seven now, and she couldn't remember whether it was five or six years since she had last slept with a man—either way, it didn't matter. She was not her sister, greedy and amoral, craving the shallow satisfaction of the excitement of sex with strangers.

Her sister—to whom the man now waiting for her response had been married. She was surprised that Eloise had cheated on him. She would have thought that he was just Eloise's type: good-looking, sexy, rich, and in a position to give her the status she and their grandfather had always craved.

Ionanthe might have acknowledged that she would never fulfil her dream of meeting a man who could be her true partner in life and in love, but she still had that same teenage longing to change the world—and for the better. That goal could now be within her reach. Through her son—the son this man would demand from her in payment of her family's debt to him—she could change the lives of her people for the better. Was that perhaps not just her fate but more importantly her destiny? That she should provide the people with a ruler who would be worthy of them?

The sun was dying into the sea, burnishing it dark gold. Ionanthe shook back her hair, the action tightening her throat, the last of the light carving her profile into a perfect cameo.

There was a pride about her, a wildness, an energy, a challenge about her, that unleashed within him an unfamiliar need to respond. Max frowned, not liking his own reaction and not really understanding it. Eloise had been sexually provocative and had left him cold. But Ionanthe challenged him with her pride, not her body or her sexuality, and for some reason his body had reacted to that. He shrugged, mentally dismissing what he did not want to dwell on. Ionanthe was a beautiful woman, and he was a man who had been without sex for almost a year.

Ionanthe turned away from the window and looked at Max.

'And if I refuse?' she demanded, her head held high, pride in every line of her body.

'You already know the answer to that. I cannot force you to marry me, but, according to my ministers and courtiers, if I do not show myself to the people as a worthy ruler by taking you, and if you do not submit to me in blood payment for the dishonour and shame your sister has brought on both our houses, then the people may very well take it upon themselves to exact payment from *you*.'

The starkness of his warning hung between them in the stern watching silence of the tower—a place that had held and held again against the enemies of the rulers of Fortenegro, protecting their lives and their honour.

The blood left Ionanthe's face, but she didn't weaken. Just the merest whisper of an exhaled breath and the movement of her throat as she swallowed betrayed what she felt.

She was as spoiled and arrogant as her sister, of course. They shared the same blood and the same up-bringing, after all, and like her sister and her grandfa-ther she would despise his plans for her country. But she had courage, Max admitted.

'I expect that it was Count Petronius who suggested that you bully me into agreeing by threatening to hand me over to the people,' she said scornfully. 'He and my grandfather were bitter enemies, who vied to have the most control over whoever sat on the throne.'

'It *was* Count Petronius who told me that in some of the more remote parts of the island the people have been known to stone adulterous wives,' Max agreed.

They looked at one another.

She was *not* going to weaken or show him any fear, Ionanthe told herself.

'I am not an adulterous wife. And I am not a posses-sion to be used to pay off my family's supposed debt to you to save your pride and your honour.' Her voice dripped acid contempt.

'This isn't about my pride or my honour,' Max cor-rected her coldly.

Ionanthe gave a small shrug, the action revealing the

smooth golden flesh of one bare shoulder as the wide boat neckline of her top slipped to one side. She felt its movement but disdained to adjust the neckline. She wasn't going to have him thinking that the thought of him looking at her bare flesh made her feel uncomfortable.

She was an outstandingly alluring woman, Max acknowledged, and yet for all her obvious sensuality she seemed unaware of its power, wearing what to other women would be the equivalent of a priceless *haute couture* garment as carelessly as though it were no more than a pair of chainstore jeans.

If she was oblivious to her effect on his sex, he was not, Max admitted. There had been women who had shared his life and his bed—beautiful, enticing women from whom he had always parted without any regret, having enjoyed a mutual satisfying sexual relationship. But none of them had ever aroused him by the sight of a bared shoulder. Merely feasting his gaze on her naked shoulder felt as erotic as though he had actually touched her skin, stroked his hand over it, absorbing its texture and its warmth.

Angered by his own momentary weakness, Max looked away from her. His life was complicated enough already, without him adding any further complications to it. Certainly it would be easier and would make more sense to let her think that he expected her to provide him with a son than to try to tell her the truth, Max acknowledged.

'The people are anxious for me to secure the succession,' he told her, his voice clipped.

The succession. Her son. The key that would unlock the medieval prison in which the people were trapped.

'My grandfather would say that it is my duty to do as you ask and take my sister's place.'

'And what do *you* say?' Max prompted.

'I say that a man who tricks and traps a woman into marriage and threatens her with death by stoning if she refuses is not a man I could either respect or honour. But you are not merely a man, are you? You are Fortenegro's ruler—its Prince.'

Even as she spoke a powerful sense of destiny was filling her. A demand. And her own answer to it rose up inside her and would not be denied. A sacrifice was being demanded of her, but the thought of the potential benefit for her people was so filled with hope and joy that her own heart filled with them as well.

She took a deep breath, and told Max calmly, 'I will marry you. But I will live my own life within that marriage. No, before you make any accusation, I do not wish to copy my sister and crawl into the beds of an endless succession of men. But there is a life I wish to live of my own, and I *shall* live it.'

'What kind of life?' Max demanded. But she refused to answer him, simply shaking her head instead.

As Max's wife, as Crown Princess, she could surely begin to do some of those things she had argued so passionately for her grandfather to do, which he had told her so angrily he would *never* do nor allow her to do either. She could start on their own estates; she would have the money. Her grandfather had been a wealthy man, and had had power. Education for the children, better working conditions for their parents— there was so much she wanted to do. But she must move carefully; she could, after all, do nothing until they were married.

Why was he standing here feeling such a sense of loss, such a sense of a darkness within himself? Ionanthe had given him the answer he needed.

Yes, she had given him that—but he sensed that there was something she was concealing from him, some sense of purpose, something that might affect his own plans to their detriment.

Max shrugged aside his doubts. Their marriage was as necessary to him for his purpose as it was to her for her safety. They would both gain something from it— just as they would both lose something.

'So we are agreed, then?' he asked her. 'You understand that you are to take your late sister's place in my life and in my bed, as my wife and the mother of my heir?'

They were stark and dispassionate words, cold words that described an equally cold marriage, Max acknowledged. But they were words that had to be said. There must be no misunderstanding on her part as to what would be expected of her.

Ionanthe lifted her chin, and told him firmly, 'Yes. I do.'

'Very well, then,' he acknowledged.

They looked at one another: two people who neither trusted nor liked one another but who understood that their future lay together and that they were trapped in it together.

CHAPTER THREE

'*ASHEEE*—how cruel it is that your poor mother did not live to see this day. Her daughter marrying our Prince and being crowned Princess.'

'I too wish that my mother was still alive, Maria,' Ionanthe told the old lady who had been part of her grandfather's household for as long as Ionanthe could remember.

She had the happiest of memories of her parents, who had died in a skiing accident in Italy when she had been thirteen. She had missed them desperately then and she still missed them now. Especially at times like this. She felt very alone, standing here in what had once been her grandfather's state apartment. The weight of the fabric of the cloth-of-gold over-dress—a priceless royal heirloom in which all Fortenegro brides were supposed to be married but which apparently her sister had refused point-blank to wear—was heavy, and felt all the more so because of the old scents of rose and lavender that clung to it, reminding her of previous brides who had worn it. But its weight was easier to bear right now than the weight of the responsibility she was about to take on—for her country and its people, she told herself fiercely, for them and for the son she would give them, who would transform their lives with the light of true democracy.

There was a heavy knock on the closed double doors, which were flung open to reveal the Lord Chamberlain in his formal regalia, flanked by heralds wearing the Prince's livery and supported by the island's highest ranking dignitaries, also wearing their ancient formal regalia.

The gold dress, worn over a rich cream lace gown that matched her veil, no longer seemed so garishly rich now that she was surrounded by her bridal escort in their scarlet, and gold.

Since she had no male relative it was the Lord Chamberlain who escorted her. The heavy weight of her skirt and his cloak combined to make a surging sound as they walked ceremoniously through the open doors of the staterooms.

Max looked down at the bent head of his bride as she knelt before him in the traditional symbolic gesture that was part of the royal marriage service whilst the Archbishop married them.

It made her blood boil to have to kneel to her new husband like this, but she must think of the greater good and not her own humiliation, Ionanthe told herself as one of the other two officiating bishops wafted the sacred scented incense over her and the other dropped gold-painted rose petals on her.

'Let the doors be thrown open and the news be carried to the furtherest part of his kingdom that the

Prince is married,' the Archbishop intoned. 'Let the trumpets sound and great joy be amongst the people.'

From her kneeling position Ionanthe couldn't see the doors being opened, but she could see the light that poured into the cathedral.

Max reached down and took hold of Ionanthe's hands, which were still folded in front of her.

Ionanthe looked up at him, ignoring the warning she had been given that it was forbidden by tradition for her to look at her new husband until he gave her permission to do so.

Also according to tradition she was now supposed to kiss his foot in gratitude for being married to him. Ionanthe's lips compressed as she deliberately stood up so that they were standing facing one another. The triumph she had been feeling at breaking with tradition and showing her own strength of character and will was lost in the Archbishop's hissed gasp of shocked breath when Max stepped forward, clasping her shoulders and holding her imprisoned as he bent his head towards her.

When she realised what he intended to do Ionanthe stiffened in rejection and hissed, 'No—you must not kiss me. It is not the tradition.'

'Then we will make our own new tradition,' Max told her equably.

His lips felt warm against her own, warm and firm and knowingly confident in a way that her own were not. They were alternately trembling and then parting, in helpless disarray. He had undermined her attempt to establish her independence far too effectively for her to be able to rally and fight back. His lips left hers and then returned, brushing them softly.

If she hadn't known better she might even have thought that his touch was meant to be reassuring—but that couldn't possibly be so, since he was the one who had mocked her with his kiss in the first place. Had he perhaps confused her with Eloise, assuming that she was like her sister and would welcome this promise of future intimacy between them? If so he was going to be in for a shock when he discovered that she did not have her sister's breadth of sexual experience. It was too late now to regret not taking advantage of the ample opportunities over the years when she had preferred her studies and her dreams to the intimacies she had been offered.

'It is not the custom for the Crown Prince's bride to stand at his side as his equal until she has asked for permission to do so,' the Archbishop was saying, with disapproval.

'Sometimes custom has to give way to a more modern way of doing things,' Ionanthe heard Max saying, before she could react herself and refuse to kneel. 'And this is one of those occasions.'

'It is our custom,' the Archbishop was insisting stubbornly.

'Then it must be changed for a new custom—one that is based on equality.'

Ionanthe knew that she was probably looking as shocked as the Archbishop, although for a different reason. The last thing she had expected was to hear her new husband talking about equality.

The Archbishop looked crestfallen and upset. 'But, sire....'

Max frowned as he listened to the quaver in the older man's voice. He had told himself that he would take things slowly and not risk offending his people, but the sight of Ionanthe kneeling at his feet had filled him with so much revulsion that he hadn't been able to stop himself from saying something.

The Archbishop's pride had been hurt, though, and he must salve that wound, Max recognised. In a more gentle voice he told him, 'I do not believe that it is fitting for the mother of my heir to kneel at any man's feet.'

The Archbishop nodded his head and looked appeased.

The new Prince was a dangerously clever man, Ionanthe decided as Max took her arm, so that together they walked down the aisle towards the open doors of the cathedral and the state carriage waiting to take them back to the palace.

An hour later they stood on the main balcony of the palace, looking down into the square where people had gathered to see them.

'At least the people are pleased to see us married. Listen to them cheering,' said Max.

'Are they cheering as loudly as they did when you married Eloise?' Ionanthe couldn't resist asking cynically. She regretted the words as soon as they had been uttered. They reminded her too sharply of the way she had felt as a child, knowing that their grandfather favoured her sister and always trying and failing to claim some of his attention and approval—some of his love—for herself. Her words had been a foolish mistake. After all, she didn't want anything from this man who had been her sister's husband.

'That was different,' he answered her quietly.

Different? Different in what way? Different because he had actually *loved* her wayward sister?

The feeling exploding inside her couldn't possibly be pain, Ionanthe denied to herself. Why should it be?

The scene down below them was one of pageantry and excitement. The square was busy with dancers in national dress, the Royal Guard in their uniforms—sentries in dark blue, gunners in dark green coats with gold braid standing by their cannons, whilst the cavalry were wearing scarlet. The rich colours stood out against the icing-white glare of the eighteenth-century baroque frontage that had been put on the old castle.

The church clock on the opposite side of the square, which had fascinated her as a child, was still drawing crowds of children to stand at the bottom, waiting for midday to strike and set off the mechanical scenes that took place one after the other. Eloise had always been far more interested in watching the changing of the guard than looking at the clock.

Ionanthe closed her eyes. She and her sister had never been close, but that did not mean she did not feel any discomfort at all at the thought of taking what had been her place. Tonight, when she lay in Max's arms fulfilling her sacrificial role, would he be thinking of Eloise? Would he be comparing her to her sister and finding her wanting? They would have been well matched in bed, her sister and this man who somehow remained very sensual and male despite the formality of the dress uniform he was wearing. It caused her a sharp spike of disquiet to know that it was his sensuality, his sexuality, that was somehow foremost in her mind, and not far more relevant aspects of his personality.

Max watched the crowd down below them, laughing happily and enjoying themselves as they celebrated their marriage—the same crowd that, according to the Count, would have threatened to depose him if he had not followed the island's tradition and accepted its cruel ancient laws. Once again he had a wife—this time one who had been blackmailed and forced into marrying him. Max wished he knew Ionanthe better. Eloise had never talked about her sister or to her, as far as Max knew, other than to say that Ionanthe had always been jealous of her because their grandfather had loved her more than he did Ionanthe.

Had he known her better, had he been able to trust her, then he might have talked openly and honestly to her. He might have told her that he loathed the way she had been forced into marriage with him as much as she did herself. Told her that as soon as it was within his power to do so he would set her free. And, had he thought there was the remotest chance that she would understand them, he might have revealed his dreams and hopes for their people to her. But he did not know her, and he could not trust her, so he could say nothing. It was too much of a risk. After all, he had already made one mistake in thinking he could trust her sister.

In the early days of their marriage, when he had still been foolish enough to think that they could work together to create a marriage based on mutual respect and a shared goal, he had talked to Eloise about his plans. She had sulked and complained that he was being boring, telling him that she thought he should let her grandfather and the other barons deal with the people, because all she wanted to do was have fun. Eloise had quickly grown bored with their marriage once she'd realised that he was not prepared to accede to her demands that they become part of the spoiled wealthy and well-born European social circle she loved.

Max had soon come to understand that there was no point in blaming Eloise for his own disillusionment at her shallowness and her adultery. The blame lay with their very different assumptions and beliefs, and the fact that they had each assumed that the other felt as they did about key issues.

Eloise and Ionanthe had been brought up in the same household, and whilst Ionanthe might *seem* to have very different values from those of her sister, that did not mean that he could trust her. As he had already discovered, the elite of the island—of which Ionanthe was a member—were fiercely opposed to the changes Max wanted to make. Given that, it made sense for him not to say anything to her.

Count Petronius appeared at Max's elbow. 'The people are waiting for you to walk amongst them to present your bride to them and receive their congratulations,' he informed them both.

Max frowned, and told him curtly, 'I don't think that would be a good idea.'

Ionanthe drew in a sharp breath on another fierce stab

of angry pride. Before she could stop herself she was demanding, 'I presume that you followed the custom when you married Eloise? That you were happy to present *her* to the people?'

How many times as a child had she been forced into the shadows whilst her grandfather proudly showed off Eloise? How many times had she been hurt by his preference for her sister? Those he had appointed to care for them had pursed their lips and shaken their heads, telling her that she was 'difficult' and that it was no wonder her grandfather preferred her prettier and 'nicer' sister. The feelings she had experienced then surged through her now, overwhelming adult logic and understanding. For a handful of seconds her new husband's unwillingness to present her to the people with pride in their relationship became her grandfather's cruel rejection of her, and she was filled with the same hurting pain as she had been then.

But analysing logically just why she should feel this angry rush of painful emotion would have to wait until she was calmer. Right now what she wanted more than anything else was recognition of her right to be respected as her sister had been.

Max's clipped 'That was different' only inflamed rather than soothed her anger.

Gritting her teeth, Ionanthe told him fiercely, 'I will not be humiliated and shamed before the people by being bundled out of sight. I may not be the bride—the wife—of your free choice, but you are the one who has forced this marriage on both of us. In marrying you I have paid my family's debt to you and to the people. I am now their Princess. They have a right to welcome me as such, and I have a right to that welcome.'

She spoke well and with pride, Max recognised, and maybe the fears he had for her safety amongst a crowd who not so very long ago might have turned on her in fury and revenge were unnecessary. She, after all, would know the people, the way they thought and felt, far better than he.

'The Princess is right, Highness. The people will expect you both to walk amongst them.'

'Very well, then,' Max agreed.

The square was crowded, the air warm from the many food stalls offering hot food. The heavy weight of the gold overdress added to Ionanthe's growing discomfort as they made their slow and stately progress through the crowd.

Initially, when they had set out from the palace steps, they had been surrounded by uniformed palace guards, but the square was packed with people and gradually they had broken through the ranks of the guards. The people might be enjoying themselves, but Ionanthe couldn't help contrasting their general air of shabbiness and poverty with the extreme richness of the appearance of those connected with the court—including, of course, herself. Here and there amongst the sea of faces, Ionanthe recognised people from her grandfather's estate, and a wave of self-revulsion washed over her as she acknowledged that *her* family was responsible for their poverty. That must change. She was determined on that.

A courtier was throwing coins into the crowd for the children, and it filled Ionanthe with anger to see them scrabbling for the money. Right in front of them one small child burst into tears as an older child wrenched open his chubby hand to remove the coins inside it. The small scene wrenched at Ionanthe's heart. Automatically she stepped forward, wanting to comfort the smaller child, but to her astonishment Max beat her to it, going down on one knee in the dust of the square to take the hands of both children. To the side of him the families looked on, their faces tight with real fear. Cosmo had treated the poorest amongst the people particularly badly, Ionanthe knew, raising taxes and punishing them for all manner of small things, laughing and saying that they were free to leave the island and live elsewhere if they did not like the way he ran his own country.

Obedient to Max's grip on their wrists, both children opened their hands. Max felt his heart contract with angry pity as he looked down at the small coins that had caused the fracas. A few pennies, that was all, and yet—as he already knew from studying the island's financial affairs—for some of the poorest families a few pennies would be vitally important. One day, if he was successful, no child on Fortenegro would need to fight for pennies or risk going hungry.

Sharing the coins between the two children equally, he closed their palms over them and then stood up, announcing firmly, 'My people—in honour of this day, every family in Fortenegro will receive the sum of one hundred *fortens*.'

Immediately a loud buzz of excitement broke out as the news was passed from person to person. The Count looked aghast and complained, 'Such a gesture will cost the treasury dear, Highness.'

'Then let it. The Treasury can certainly afford it; it is less, I suspect, than my late cousin would have spent on the new yacht he was planning to commission.'

There were tears of real gratitude in the eyes of the people listening to him, and Ionanthe could feel her own eyes starting to smart with emotion as she reacted to his unexpected generosity. But he was still Cosmo's cousin, she reminded herself fiercely. Still the same man who had threatened and forced her into this marriage with him rather than risk losing his royal status and everything that went with it. One act of casual kindness could not alter that.

It appalled and shocked her to realise how easily swayed her emotions were; in some way she seemed to want to believe the best of him, as though she was already emotionally vulnerable to him. That was ridiculous—more than ridiculous. It was impossible. The emotion she felt stemmed from her concern for the people, that was all, and she must make sure he knew it.

When the Count had turned away, she lifted her chin and told Max fiercely, 'It is all very well giving them money, but what they really need is the freedom to earn a decent wage instead of working for a pittance as they do now for the island's rich landowners.'

'One of which was your grandfather,' Max pointed out coolly. Her words stung.

What had he expected? He derided himself. That she

would turn to him and praise him for his actions? That she would look at him with warmth in her eyes instead of contempt? That she would fling herself into his arms? Of course not. Why should it matter *what* she thought of him? She was simply a means to an end, that was all. A means to an end and yet a human being whose freedom of choice was being sacrificed to appease an age-old custom. For the greater good, Max insisted to himself—against his conscience.

'It is time, I think, for us to head back to the palace.'

Delicate, but oh-so-erotic shivers of pleasure slid wantonly over Ionanthe's skin in the place where Max's warm breath had touched it. Her reaction took her completely off guard. Shock followed pleasure—shock that her body was capable of having such an immediate and intense reaction to any man, but most of all to this one. It was totally out of character for her—totally unfamiliar, totally unwanted and unacceptable—and yet still her flesh was clinging to the memory of the sensation it had soaked up so greedily. She had gone years without missing or wanting a man's sensual touch—so why now, as though some magical button had been pressed, was she becoming so acutely aware of this man's sensuality?

Infuriated with herself for her weakness, Ionanthe moved out of reach of a second assault on her defences, firmly reminding herself of the reality of the situation. This was a man who was already dictating to her and telling her what to do. To him she was merely a possession—payment of a debt he was owed. And tonight in his arms she would have to make the first payment.

A shudder tore through her. She should not have allowed herself to think of that, of tonight.

As she moved away from him he reached out to stop her, placing his hand on her arm. Even though he wasn't using any force, and even though her arms were covered, thanks to her unwanted heightened state of awareness she could feel each one of his fingers pressing on her as though there was no barrier between them. His touch was that of flesh on flesh. Disturbing and unwanted images slid serpent-like into her mind— images of him with her sister, touching her, caressing her, admiring and praising her. Once again emotion spiked sharply through her, reminding her of the jealousy she had felt as a child. This was so wrong, so foolish, and so dangerous. She was *not* competing with her dead sister for this man's approval. There was only one thing she wanted from him and it was not his sexual desire for her. The only reason she had married him was the people of Fortenegro, for the son who would one day rule benignly over them. For that she was prepared to undergo and endure whatever was necessary. She pulled away from him, plunging into the crowd, determined to show him her independence.

'Ionanthe! No!' Max protested, cursing under his breath as she was swallowed up by the crowd, and forcing his way through it after her.

People were pressing in on her, the crowd was carrying her along with it, almost causing her to lose her balance. Fear stabbed through Ionanthe as she realised how vulnerable she was in her heavy clothes.

An elderly man grabbed hold of her arm, warning

her, 'You had better do better by our Prince than that whore of a sister of yours. She shamed us all when she shamed him.'

Spittle flecked his lips, and his eyes were wild with anger as he shook her arm painfully. The people surrounding her who had been smiling before were now starting to frown, their mood changing. She looked round for the guards but couldn't see any of them. She was alone in a crowd which was quickly becoming hostile to her.

She hadn't thought it was in her nature to panic, but she was beginning to do so now.

Then Ionanthe felt another hand on her arm, in a touch that extraordinarily her body somehow recognised. And a familiar voice was saying firmly, 'Princess Ionanthe has already paid the debt owed by her family to the people of Fortenegro. Her presence here today as my bride and your Princess is proof of that.'

He was at her side now, his presence calming the crowd and forcing the old man to release her, as the crowd began to murmur their agreement to his words.

Calmly but determinedly Max was guiding her back through the crowd. A male voice called out to him from the crowd.

'Make sure you get us a fine future prince on her as soon as maybe, Your Highness.' The sentiment was quickly taken up by others, who threw in their own words of bawdy advice to the new bridegroom. Ionanthe fought to stop her face from burning with angry humiliated colour. Torn between unwanted relief that she had been rescued and discomfort about what was being said,

Ionanthe took refuge in silence as they made their way back towards the palace.

They had almost reached the main entrance when once again Max told hold of her arm. This time she fought against her body's treacherous reaction, clamping down on the sensation that shot through her veins and stiffening herself against it. The comments she had been subjected to had brought home to her the reality of what she had done; they clung inside her head, rubbing as abrasively against her mind as burrs would have rubbed against her skin.

'Isn't it enough for you to have forced me into marrying you? Must you force me to obey your will physically as well?' she challenged him bitterly.

Max felt the forceful surge of his own anger swelling through him to meet her biting contempt, shocking him with its intensity as he fought to subdue it.

Not once during the months he had been married to Eloise had she ever come anywhere near arousing him emotionally in the way that Ionanthe could, despite the fact that he had known her only a matter of days. She seemed to delight in pushing him—punishing him for their current situation, no doubt, he reminded himself as his anger subsided. It was completely out of character for him to let anyone get under his skin enough to make him react emotionally to them when his response should be purely cerebral.

'Far from wishing to force you to do anything, I merely wanted to suggest that we use the side entrance to the palace. That way we will attract less attention.'

He had a point, Ionanthe admitted grudgingly, but

she wasn't going to say so. Instead she started to walk towards the door set in one of the original castle turrets, both of them slipping through the shadows the building now threw across the square, hidden from the view of the people crowding the palace steps. She welcomed the peace of its stone interior after the busyness of the square. Her dress had become uncomfortably heavy and her head had started to ache. The reality of what she had done had begun to set in, filling her with a mixture of despair and panic. But she mustn't think of herself and her immediate future, she told herself as she started to climb the stone steps that she knew from memory led to a corridor that connected the old castle to the more modern palace.

She had almost reached the last step when somehow or other she stepped onto the hem of her gown, the accidental movement unbalancing her and causing her to stumble. Max, who was several steps below her, heard the small startled sound she made and raced up the stairs, catching her as she fell.

If she was trembling with the fragility of new spring buds in the wind then it was because of her shock. If she felt weak and her heart was pounding with dangerous speed then it was because of the weight of her gown. If she couldn't move then it was because of the arms that imprisoned her.

She had to make him release her. It was dangerous to be in his arms. She looked up at him, her gaze travelling the distance from his chin to his mouth and then refusing to move any further. What had been a mere tremor of shock had now become a fiercely violent shudder that came from deep within her and ached through her. She felt dizzy, light-headed, removed from everything about herself she considered 'normal'. She had become, instead, a woman who hungered for something unknown and forbidden.

Was this how her sister had felt with those men, those strangers, she had delighted in taking to her bed? Hungering for something she knew she should not want? It was a disturbing thought. She had always prided herself on being different from Eloise, on having different values from the sister, whose behaviour she had never been able to relate to and had privately abhorred.

It was because her heart was racing so fast that his own had started to pound heavily, Max told himself. It was because the walls either side of the steps enclosed them that he was so conscious of the scent of her hair and her skin. It was because he was a man and she was a woman that his body was flooded with an unwanted surge of physical arousal that had him tightening his hold on her.

He wanted her, Max knew. The knowledge rushed over him and through him, possessing him as he ached to possess her, threatening to carry with it every moral barrier and code that should have held it back. Why? It was illogical, unfathomable, the opposite of so much about himself he had believed unchangeable. He felt as though he had stepped outside his own skin and become a hostage to his own need in a way that filled him with mental distaste and rejection. Yet at the same time his body renewed its assault on those feelings as though it was determined to have its way.

To travel so far and in such an unfamiliar direction so unexpectedly and in so short a space of time had robbed him of the ability to think logically, Max decided.

An aeon could have passed, or merely a few seconds. She was quite unable to judge the difference, Ionanthe admitted, because she was too caught up in the maelstrom of sensations and emotions that had somehow been created out of nothing and which were still controlling her. And would probably continue to control her for as long as Max was holding her. She was quite literally spellbound, and he was the one who had cast that spell, binding her senses to his will, forcing from them a response she would never willingly have given him, stirring up within her a dark mystery of maddening longing that had seized and held captive her ability to think or reason.

All she knew was that his lips were only a sigh away from her own. All she wanted to know was the possession of them on her own. There was nothing else in this moment but him.

The normal Ionanthe—the Ionanthe she knew— would never have closed her eyes and swayed closer to Max, exhaling on a breath that was a siren's call. But this Ionanthe was not her normal self. This Ionanthe was not prepared to listen to any objections from its alter ego.

He should resist. Max knew that. This trick of pretended longing and faked intimacy had been one of Eloise's favourites, and it had been a ploy he had found easy enough to withstand when she'd used it against him. Somehow, though, with Ionanthe things were different. Her lips, soft and warm with natural colour, were surely shaped for kisses and sensuality. They pillowed the touch of his own, igniting within him a need that roared through him like a forest fire.

Extreme danger. How often had she heard those words and dismissed them and those who lived to experience it, those who holidayed in places that offered it? Now she could only marvel that they should go to such lengths when all the time it was here, so close at hand, in a man's arms and beneath the hard pressure of his lips.

Extreme danger and extreme desire went hand in hand, producing between them an extreme pleasure that was an almost unbearable delight. A delight that was merely a foretaste of what the night that lay before them would hold for her. How could Eloise have wanted someone else when she'd had a husband who could give her this kind of pleasure?

Eloise! Abruptly Ionanthe pulled back from Max before he could stop her, telling him in a voice designed to conceal the shaky vulnerability she was really feeling, 'My sister may have welcomed being treated like a sex object, but I don't.'

Her angry contempt coming hard on the heels of her earlier eagerness rasped against Max's already dangerously charged emotions. How the hell had he managed to lose control of himself so easily and so quickly?

'You could have fooled me,' he responded grimly. 'In fact I'd have gone as far as to say you were positively…'

'What? Asking for it? Is that what you were going to say?' Ionanthe rounded on him angrily. 'How typical of a man like you—but then I suppose I shouldn't have expected anything else. Cosmo was a sexist bully, and you are obviously cut from the same cloth.'

Her accusation cooled Max's own anger to sharp-edged ice.

'What I was going to say was that you seemed to be positively enjoying it. But if we're talking about shared family flaws, then perhaps *I* should have remembered that your sister also had a taste for playing the tease, blowing hot when she wanted something and then blowing cold when it suited her.'

I am not Eloise, Ionanthe wanted to say. But she remembered how often her grandfather had distanced himself from her and withheld his love from her with the words, 'You are not Eloise.' Instead she picked up her heavy skirts and turned her back on Max as she headed down the empty corridor.

CHAPTER FOUR

SHE was free now of the presence of the stiffly correct lady's maid she had needed to help her out of the heavy formality of her wedding gown, alone in the bedroom she would be sharing with her new husband.

Over the handful of days that had elapsed between Max presenting her with his ultimatum and their marriage Ionanthe had told both Max and the Count that she did not want to be surrounded by ladies-in-waiting or a large staff, and it had eventually been agreed that two ladies-in-waiting would attend her on only the most formal occasions, and that she would have only one personal maid who would attend her only when she needed her.

It was a relief to be wearing her own clothes again—even if the maid had eyed them with disdain.

The suite of rooms she was to share with Max had surprised her. She had assumed that he would be occupying the Royal State Apartments, which she remembered from her childhood, but Max had created his own far more modern living quarters in the older part of the building—the castle itself—rather than opting to live in the seventeenth-century addition of the palace. The 'new' royal apartments comprised a drawing room, a dining room with a small kitchen off it, the bedroom she was now in, two bathrooms and two dressing rooms, which were entered via doors on either side of the large bed that she was trying desperately hard to ignore.

The drawing room had large glass doors that opened out onto a private terrace, complete with an infinity swimming pool, and the view from the apartments' windows was one of wild rugged splendour over the cliffs and out to sea.

Unlike the rest of the palace, with its grand and formal decor and furniture, these rooms had a much more modern and relaxed air to them. In fact they were rooms in which she would have felt very much at home in other circumstances.

She had deliberately chosen to change into a pair of jeans and a simple tee shirt, as though wearing them was somehow like wearing a badge of independence, making a statement about what she was and what she was not. And because she wanted to distance herself in every way from what had happened earlier, so that he knew it had been a momentary aberration—her response to him alien to everything she believed she stood for and something never to be repeated.

She did not desire him. She simply desired the son he would give her. When she lay beneath him, enduring the possession of his body, it would be because of her belief that the people on this island deserved to be freed from their servitude. Not because she wanted to be there, and certainly not because she gloried in being there. There would be no repetition of that earlier kiss. She would show him no weakness or vulnerability.

Abruptly she realised that she was pacing the floor. Why? She already knew that he would claim payment of her family's debt to him. If he thought to draw out her torment by making her wait, because he thought she would be anxious until it was over and done with, then she would show him that he was wrong.

She opened the glass doors and stepped out onto the terrace. The air on this side of the island smelled and felt different, somehow—sharper, stronger, more exhilarating. The sea both protected the castle and reminded those who had built it that it was a dangerous restless living force that could never be ignored. Like love itself.

Love? What had *that* to do with anything?

Everything, she told herself sombrely. Because she would love the son this marriage would bring her, and in turn would ensure that he loved his people.

Late autumn had long ago faded into winter and now the tops of the mountains that lay inland were capped with snow as icy and remote as the heart of this marriage she had made.

Where was he? When was he going to come to her and demand his pound of flesh? Ionanthe paced the terrace as she looked towards the bedroom she would have to share with Max.

At least it was not the same bedchamber he had shared with her sister. Yania, the young woman who had been appointed to attend her, had told her that when she had mentioned that Max had moved out of the Royal State Apartments immediately after Eloise's death.

Because he couldn't bear to sleep there alone without her?

What did it matter to her *what* he felt?

She turned round to stare out to sea.

'I'm sorry. I got involved in some necessary paperwork which took longer than I had anticipated.'

Was it the fact that she hadn't heard him come towards her or the fact that she hadn't expected his apology that was causing her heart to thump so unsteadily against her chest wall?

'Have you eaten? Are you hungry?'

'No, and no,' Ionanthe answered him shortly, adding, 'Look, we both know what we're here for, so why don't we just get it over with?'

Max frowned. Her dismissive, almost critical manner was so different from the come-on she had given him earlier that it struck him that it must be just another ploy—and that irritated him. He'd expected anger, resentment, bitterness—those were the things he had been prepared for her to display, the things he'd promised himself he'd try to find a way to soothe for both their sakes. Fiery, ardent passion followed by icy disdain were not. She was challenging his pride, needling him into a retaliation he couldn't subdue.

'"Get it over with"?' he repeated grimly. 'Are you sure that's what you really want?'

He was referring to that…that incident on the stairs, Ionanthe knew, trying to humiliate and mock her because of her response to him then. The memory of that response was a taste as sour as the bitter aloes her nursemaid had painted on her nails as a child to stop her from biting them. Ionanthe looked down at those nails now, immaculately neat, with well-shaped cuticles, buffed to a soft natural sheen.

Max saw Ionanthe look down at her own hand. Her nails were free of the polish with which Eloise had always painted hers, and he had a sudden urge to reach for her hand, with its slim wrist and elegant fingers, and hold it within his own in an age-old gesture of comfort. Comfort? For her or for himself? Why not for both of them? After all, they were entering the unknown and uncertain world their marriage would be together, weren't they?

What was wrong with him? He already knew that there could be no real intimacy between them. Far better that they kept their emotional distance from one another. After all, she had made it plain enough to him that she didn't look for anything from their physical union other than getting it 'over with.'

He had moved closer to her, Ionanthe recognised. She hadn't seen him move, but her body knew that he had. Her senses had registered it and were still registering it; her nerve-endings were going into overload as they relayed back the effect his closeness was having on them.

'Yes. That is what I want,' Ionanthe confirmed, her pride pushing her to add recklessly, 'What else is there for me to want?'

'Pleasure, perhaps?' Max suggested.

Pleasure. Her muscles locked against the images his mocking words had evoked, but it was too late. Those same feelings she had experienced on the steps were running riot inside her like a gang of skilled pickpockets, overturning the barriers put up to deter them and plundering the vulnerable cache they had discovered.

'I don't look for pleasure in a relationship such as ours.' Her words were as much a denial of what she could feel within her own body as they were of what she was sure was his taunting mockery of her.

'But if you were to find it there…' Max persisted.

'That's impossible. There could never be any pleasure for me in having sex with a man I can't respect. I wouldn't want there to be. It would shame me to want such a man,' she declared furiously, desperate to stop him from thinking she had actually wanted him when they had shared that kiss.

Max felt the swift running tide of his own pride, its power and speed sucking away reason and impartiality. She was challenging him as a man—challenging his ability to arouse her and pleasure her. Telling him that she would rather lie ice-cold in his arms than permit her body to be warmed by any shared need or desire.

Ionanthe saw the glint of anger in Max's eyes. A quiver of something that was more than mere apprehension feathered across her nerves. Perhaps she had gone too far? she admitted. Said more than was wise? Now, in the chill of her growing anxiety, it was easy to admit what she had not been prepared to see in the heat of her prideful anger. Her husband was a powerful, sexual man—a man who knew how to touch a woman's body to draw the most sensual response from it. In her determination to stop him from thinking that she wanted him, and so spare her pride, had she unwittingly triggered his own pride?

'I am sure we are both agreed that we have in our different ways made a commitment that it is our duty to honour,' Ionanthe told Max hastily, trying to repair the damage she feared she might have caused. 'That being the case, I am sure we are also agreed that there is no need for either of us to look for anything more than the…the satisfaction that comes from doing that duty.'

'Your views on sex are obviously very different from those of your late sister,' Max responded wryly.

'My views on many things differ from those of Eloise,' Ionanthe hit back. 'I did not want to marry you,' she added when he made no response. 'You were the one who forced me into this marriage.'

'You are right,' Max announced. 'We might as well "get it over with".'

Was it because he was thinking about Eloise, comparing her sexuality to her late sister's and finding her wanting that he had made that abrupt statement? Ionanthe wondered.

The light had faded whilst they had been arguing, the sun sinking down into the sea and turning it a dull molten gold.

In their absence an ice bucket containing a bottle of champagne and two crystal champagne flutes had been placed on one of the modern black-marble-topped tables just inside the glass doors.

Ionanthe watched as Max opened the bottle with a single economically fluid movement, expertly filling the two glasses and then holding one out to her.

She rarely drank, but she suspected that to refuse

now would open her up to another unfavourable comparison with her late sister.

'What shall we toast?' Max asked as she took the glass from him.

What did you toast on your wedding night with Eloise? Ionanthe was tempted to ask, but of course she didn't. Instead she looked at him and said quietly, 'I would toast freedom. But of course it is not a toast we can share.'

Max could feel the anger burning up under his skin.

'You toast freedom, then, and I shall toast pleasure,' he told her mockingly, slanting a glance at her that made her whole body burn.

She was trembling so much she could barely hold the glass, never mind drink from it.

When she replaced it on the table, Max said coolly, 'You're right—we're wasting time when we should be performing our duty.' He shot back his cuff and looked at his watch—a plain, serviceable watch, not at all the kind of ostentatious rich man's toy she would have expected him to be wearing.

'Shall we agree to meet in the bedroom in, say, fifteen minutes' time? Dressed, or rather undressed for action?'

Ionanthe could feel her heart bumping along the bottom of her ribcage. She wasn't going to let him see the despair she was beginning to feel, though. Instead she lifted her chin and agreed, 'Very well.'

Max drained his glass, and was just turning away from her when after a brief knock the drawing room door was hurriedly opened. The Chancellor came in, looking very concerned, Count Petronius hard on his heels,

'I told you there was no need for us to disturb His

Highness, Ethan. I can deal with this matter,' said the Count.

'What matter?' Max demanded.

The Chancellor needed no further invitation. Ignoring the Count's obvious irritation he addressed Max. 'Highness, there has been a disturbance in the city—fighting in the streets among some of the men of your new bride's people, claiming that it is wrong that she has been forced to make a blood payment on behalf of her sister—'

'They have been arrested and are now, as we speak, being held in the square by the Royal Guard,' the Count broke in. 'There is no need for you to concern yourself on the matter, Highness. They will be treated with appropriate severity.'

'No!' Ionanthe defended her people automatically. These were men who had been loyal to her late parents and to their land. Now they stood firm to support Ionanthe. 'They will have meant no real harm.'

'They threatened the person of their ruler,' the Count insisted. 'And they must be punished accordingly.'

Max looked from the Count's implacable expression to Ionanthe's flushed face. So, *something* could apparently arouse his bride to passion, even if it wasn't him.

'I shall speak to these men myself,' he told the Count.

'And I shall come with you,' Ionanthe told them both firmly.

Max looked at her. Her announcement and her determination were very different from the reaction he had expected, knowing from experience what the reaction of both her sister and her grandfather would have been. He would have pursued the subject, to satisfy what he admitted was his growing curiosity about the differences he was observing between his late wife and the sister who had taken her place, but this was not the time for that.

'Sire, I would urge you not to risk either your own safety or that of Her Highness,' the Count was warning. 'Far better to allow the authorities to deal with the situation.'

Max listened to him, and then pointed out coolly, 'I disagree with you, Count. In fact I believe that it is time that all the people of Fortenegro recognised that *I* am this island's final authority, and that *my* word is law.'

With a brisk nod of his head, and without waiting to see what the Count's reaction was to his none-too-subtle challenge to the older man's determination to hold on to the power he had made on his own, Max strode towards the main doors to the castle.

'Open the doors,' he told the waiting guards firmly.

Was he going to order that those who were loyal to her family be punished? Ionanthe worried as she half ran to catch up with him.

'The Count is right when he says that you should not be exposed to danger,' Max told her.

'I am coming with you,' Ionanthe repeated, raising her voice so that he could hear it above the noise pouring in through the now open doors from the square below.

Somehow or other, without the need of heralds or trumpets, the crowd seemed to sense their presence, even though Max had descended the steps in silence. The words 'the Prince' seemed to pass from one person to another, to become a hush that gathered in force and intensity until the whole square was silently expectant. A shiver ran through Ionanthe as she felt the ancient power of the people's belief in and dependence on their ruler.

On the other side of the square the lights on the walls clearly illuminated the ceremonial uniforms of the Royal Guard, highlighting the disparity between their richness and the poverty of the small group of men they had herded into a corner and were keeping captive. *Her people.* A huge lump formed in Ionanthe's throat and her eyes stung with tears of mingled pity and pride for the men who had been brave enough and foolish enough to want to protect her.

Without thinking, she turned to Max and hissed fiercely, 'You must not hurt them.'

From deep within her memory she heard an echo of Cosmo as a young boy, saying savagely to her in the middle of a childhood quarrel, '*You* cannot tell me to do anything. I am Fortenegro's ruler. No one can tell me what to do, and those who try have to be punished.'

Max was ignoring her, and instead was striding towards the captives and their captors. The mass of people in the square parted before him.

When he reached the guards, Max demanded, 'What is going on here?'

'We have arrested these troublemakers, sire,' the most senior of the guards told him.

'You have forced our Duchess to marry you under duress. It is our duty to protect her and her honour,' one of the men under guard shouted.

Immediately someone in the crowd who had heard him yelled out, 'Listen to how the traitor speaks of our

Prince and the honour of a family that has no right to any honour. His words are an insult to His Highness.'

Despite herself, Ionanthe shivered as she saw the speed with which anger burned its way through the crowd.

Max saw the colour leave Ionanthe's face, and without being able to reason why he should want to do so he reached for her hand, holding it within his own and giving it a comforting squeeze.

Any prideful attempt she might have wanted to make to pull away was demolished as the crowd started to surge around them, almost knocking Ionanthe off her feet. Small stones were being thrown at the captive men.

Quickly Max pulled her close to him, holding her protectively and then commanding, 'My people, listen to me. Today has signified a very special moment in our shared history. For your sake, and out of her love for you, the Duchess Ionanthe consented to become my wife. Those who have served her family have every right to feel great pride in the sacrifice she has made for the sake of our principality. Together we will work for the good of this island and its people—all its people. It is my will and my decree that our wedding day should not be marred by violence and punishment.'

Although initially shocked to hear Max speak in such a powerful and flattering way about her, Ionanthe recovered quickly, seizing the moment to join her own voice to that of her new husband and address the now silent and watchful crowd.

'Your Prince speaks the truth.' She turned to where the captive men were standing stiffly and resentfully and told them, 'You do me great honour, but it is no exaggeration to say that your Prince has done me an even greater honour in taking me as his wife.'

A low rumble of dissent from her people and an even stronger rumble of contempt from the rest of the crowd swelled ominously into the silence, but Ionanthe refused to be deterred. She could feel the warmth of Max's arm against her back and she could feel too the protective clasp of his hand on her shoulder.

'Out of our shared love for you, if God wills it, the Prince and I will create the son who will one day rule you all. It is for him that I have submitted to my duty in the eyes of our ancient law, for him that your Prince has accepted my sacrifice. My people—our people—we do this for you.'

The whole square had fallen silent once more, but it was a tense, watchful and judging silence, Ionanthe knew. A silence that brooded and threatened. And then, unbelievably, Max caught hold of her hand and lifted it to his lips. Placing his kiss not on her knuckles but rather opening her palm and placing a kiss into it. Those close enough to witness the emotional intimacy and intensity of the small gesture gasped.

'My wife is right,' Max told the crowd. And, raising his voice, he commanded them, 'My people, this is not a time to dwell on past quarrels or injustices. It is a time to celebrate. Those who would have fought for the honour of my wife are to be praised, not punished, because in serving her best interests they also serve mine. I commend their loyalty, just as I promise my loyalty to all of you. Captain—' he turned to the captain of the Guard '—these men are to be allowed to go free.'

There was a great cheer from the crowd, and then another, and then suddenly the people were surging all around them, laughing and cheering, the earlier mood of hostility wiped clean away.

'Thank you for…for freeing them,' she managed to say to Max, even though she knew her voice was stilted.

The movement of the crowd suddenly threw Ionanthe against Max's chest. His arms came round her to hold her steady. Her hands were on his shoulders as she too sought to steady herself. She looked up at him, and then couldn't look away. The noise of the crowd seemed to fade, and all her senses registered was contained within the encirclement of Max's arms. He bent his head towards her own. Her heart was beating far too fast—and for no sensible reason. Her people were safe now, there was no need for her heart to thud or her pulse to race.

Max's lips touched her own, their possession hard and purposeful. She should pull away, she *wanted* to pull away, but the dominating power of his mouth on hers wouldn't let her. Instead she felt as though she was being carried by a swift and dangerous current that was taking her deeper with every breath she took. Until she was giving in to it and sinking down into its hot velvet darkness, allowing it to take her and possess her. Reality and everything that went with it was forgotten, sent into oblivion by what she was feeling, as though those feelings and her own senses had united against her, treacherously allowing an enemy force to overwhelm her defences.

Her whole body had turned soft and heavy, as though she had drunk some potion brewed by the witches who centuries ago were supposed to have inhabited the high mountains of Fortenegro. Desires, longings, needs that less than half an hour ago she would have fiercely claimed it was impossible for her to feel for any man, much less this one, were now burning through her, invading her belly, making her breasts ache, making her long with increasing sexual urgency for the most intense and intimate possession of her flesh by the man who was holding her.

And then the darkness beyond the town square was broken as a firework display began, the sound bringing her back to reality. Above them in the night sky showers of multi-coloured stars exploded and then fell back to earth, their effect a mere shadow of the explosion of desire inside her. Shocked, Ionanthe pulled herself out of Max's arms.

His arms felt cold and empty, and his body was racked with a physical ache that gnawed at him; all he wanted right now, Max acknowledged, was to take Ionanthe back to the castle and his bed. Her response to his kiss had ignited a need inside him that had taken him completely by surprise. And, more than that, during those intense moments a hope had come to life inside him that went against everything he had told himself he believed with regard to any marriage he might make. It should have been a salutary experience, or at the very least one which left him feeling wary and concerned about his own misjudgement, but instead what he actually felt was a feeling that was far sweeter.

Could it be that against all the odds—miraculously, almost—they shared a mutual desire for one another which could prove to be an unexpected foundation stone on which they could build a strong marriage? Max asked himself ruefully. If so… He looked at Ionanthe.

Sensing Max's gaze focusing on her, and dreading what she suspected she would see in it if she were foolish enough to meet it, Ionanthe fought to keep her burning face, with its scarlet banners advertising her folly, to herself.

She knew perfectly well what Max would be thinking. She had experienced male sexual arrogance—if mainly second hand—often enough during the course of her work in Brussels to know full well that the average man's reaction to a woman who responded as passionately as she had just done to Max was to assume that she must find him irresistible, must be desperate for even more sexual intimacy with him. There was no way Ionanthe wanted Max to think that about her. It offended her pride more than enough that she had to acknowledge to herself that she had responded to him, without having to endure *him* smirking over her vulnerability as well. She had to say something that would convince him that she had not really been affected by his kiss at all.

Ionanthe took a deep breath and said, as coolly as she could, 'Well, now that I've played my part and done everything I can to convince everyone that I've married you willingly, including that faked display of wifely adoration, perhaps we could return to the palace?'

Ionanthe took care to wait for the silence that followed with a small frosty smile that was more a baring of her pretty white teeth than a real smile, before actually risking a look at Max.

The stony expression carved on his face should have been reassuring—as should the icy-cold tones in which he informed her, in a very distancing manner, 'Very well. I'll get the Captain of the Guard to escort you back.'

Instead, for some silly reason, they actually made her feel abandoned and forlorn.

So much for his stupid hopes, Max reflected grimly as he watched the Captain of the Guard escorting Ionanthe back to the hotel. At least the Captain was a middle-aged, heavily set man, and not the kind of Adonis-like youth his first wife had seemed to find so irresistible—just in case her sister should have the same proclivities. What a fool he'd been to think for even a moment that there could be something personal between them. Hell, he'd already told himself that that was the last thing he wanted. Didn't he already have more than enough on his plate, with all the problems involved in bringing a new era to subjects without wanting to burden himself with some more? He simply could not take the risk of allowing himself to become sexually or emotionally vulnerable to Ionanthe. He knew that.

Cerebrally he might know it, but what about his body?

His body would have to learn, Max told himself grimly.

It was late in the evening—far later than he had initially envisaged having this conversation, thanks to the incident in the square—and the formal surroundings of the Grand Ministerial Chamber were hardly suited to its subject matter. But he had been determined to sign the necessary declaration that would ensure the freedom of the protestors without any delay.

Not that their earlier surroundings had been any more intimate—their first shared evening meal as a newly married couple having taken place in the equally formal and grand State Dining Room, where they had been seated at either end of a table designed to accommodate formal state dinners. With the length of a polished mahogany table that could easily seat fifty people sep-arating them, and a silver-gilt centrepiece from the Royal Treasury between them, even if they had wanted to talk to one another it would have been impossible.

However, despite the cold hauteur with which Ionanthe had made plain exactly what her expectations of their marriage were, Max felt duty bound to have this conversation.

'As there hasn't been time to arrange a formal hon-eymoon—' he began.

'I don't want one.' Ionanthe stopped him quickly.

He had taken her sister to Italy—surely one of the most romantic honeymoon venues there could be?—but that wasn't the reason for her immediate interruption. That owed its existence to what had happened to her out in the square, when Max had kissed her. How easily she had risked humiliating herself. She could just imagine how much it would please her new husband's male ego if he thought that he could arouse her so easily. Men had no conscience when it came to women's emotions and desires. She had seen that so often in Brussels. She had seen how men exploited the vulnerability of women, persuading them to give up their own moral beliefs for their own advantage. She certainly wasn't going to put herself in that position—not when there was so much at stake for the country, for the son she hoped to have who would one day rule it.

There must be no further impulsive and unnecessary intimacies between Max and herself. It was her duty to consummate their marriage—how else could she conceive the son she was so determined to have for the people?—but she was determined not to put herself in a position where she might be sucked back into that dangerous state she had experienced earlier. A cool, calm and controlled execution of her marital and royal duty was her goal.

'Maybe not,' Max agreed calmly, 'but it is expected. Therefore I plan to arrange for us to spend several days at the hunting lodge.'

Ionanthe looked at him in dismay.

The Royal Hunting Lodge was up in the mountains, and in winter doubled as a ski lodge as it was above the snow line.

'Surely it will be inconvenient for you to be away from the centre of government?' she protested. Not for anything was she going to admit to him that the hunting lodge's remoteness and the fact that they would be alone there were filling her with panic.

When Max made no response she shrugged and affected a cool logic she was far from feeling, telling him, 'I can't see any purpose in us isolating ourselves in the mountains. It is our duty, I know, to produce an heir to succeed you, but we can do that just as well here.'

Such a pragmatic and logical, unemotional approach to their union was surely something he should applaud, Max told himself. After all, it reflected everything he had already told himself their marriage must be. Why, then, was he finding that he felt not just repelled but also in some dangerous way actively challenged as a man by Ionanthe's attitude to the intimacy they must share?

'You showed great passion this evening in your defence of your people.'

Ionanthe stiffened. What was he hinting? Was he going to ask her to deny that she had also shown great passion for him? Her pride writhed in agony at the thought.

'Their safety is my responsibility,' she answered coldly. 'Your sexual pleasure is not. I refuse to fake passion for the sake of a man's ego. You may have been able to force me to marry you, but you cannot force me to desire you and nor will I do so. Having said that, however, as I have already confirmed, I am fully prepared to fulfil my duty to the crown and to the people.'

The red mist of savage male sexual anger that rose up inside him shocked Max. He had to bring this conversation to a close before he was tempted to do something he considered beneath him, something he knew ultimately he would regret. He had never before wanted to overwhelm a woman's resistance and arouse her to the point where she succumbed and gave herself completely and mindlessly to him out of the white-hot desire he had brought her to. But right now the images imposing themselves on his thoughts were of Ionanthe on a bed—a very large bed—on which their naked bodies were passionately entwined. Even without closing his eyes and focusing his senses he could imagine the silky softness of her hair against his own skin, its scent—her scent—heated by desire to release its erotic fragrance into the air, filling his nostrils. Her head would be thrown back against his arm, her eyes a passion-glazed glitter between thick dark lashes, her lips swollen from their shared kisses and eagerly parted, proclaiming her pleasure and her desire for more as she smiled invitingly up at him.

Angrily Max dragged his thoughts back to reality. He had no business allowing his mind to create such images. They were an offence, a mental assault that he could not allow to continue and that he would not tolerate in himself.

Even so, he could not stop himself from saying curtly, 'You have a very clinical and detached attitude to the creation of a new life. A child deserves to be loved by those who give it life.'

'The fact that I can remain clinical and detached about the process that will create the next ruler of Fortenegro does not mean that I will not love my son any more than a woman who seeks medical intervention in order to conceive does not love *her* child,' Ionanthe retaliated sharply.

How much longer was she going to have to wait? Lying alone in the darkness of the large bed, waiting for Max to come to her, Ionanthe tried not to feel anxious. She had promised herself that she would remain calm, that she would not repeat her foolishness of earlier in the evening, but now, with the chimes of the cathedral clock striking midnight dying into silence, it was growing harder for her to quell her over-active imagination.

What would she do if he refused to adopt the same clinical manner she had sworn to show him and instead kissed her as he had done in the square? Why was she asking herself such a silly question? If he did that, then of course she would not respond to him. But if he were to persist? If he were to persist then she must just continue to remain unaffected.

How much longer would it be before he came to her? Was he delaying deliberately, in order to torment her and to break down her resistance? Did he think by leaving her here alone in their marriage bed that when he did choose to join her she would be so grateful that she would fling herself into his arms? If so, then he was going to learn just how wrong he was.

She looked at her watch. It was half past twelve. Had her sister found him such a reluctant bridegroom? Somehow Ionanthe doubted it.

Where *was* he?

It had been a long day, but despite her physical tiredness she knew that it would be impossible for her to sleep until the final act cementing their union had been completed. Beyond the huge windows which she had deliberately asked to be left uncurtained she could see the bright sharpness of the late autumn moon. Not many weeks ago it would have had the heavy fullness of the ripe harvest moon, signalling the culmination of nature's seasons of productivity, emblazoning her fertility across the night sky. Ionanthe touched her flat stomach. There was a season for all things, for all life, a time of planting and growing. An ache sprang to life inside her, urgent and demanding: the desire for a seed that would create the most precious gift Mother Nature could give.

Tears came out of nowhere to burn the backs of her eyes, accompanied by a helpless yearning and longing. Her body was waiting to conceive this son she wanted so very much. She was ready to give herself over to the sacrifice she must make for the future of the people. More than anything else right now she wanted to feel that necessary male movement within her, giving her the spark of life she ached so physically for. It must be her longing for the conception of their child that was driving into her, possessing her, filling her with restless longing. It couldn't possibly be anything else.

Where *was* he?

CHAPTER FIVE

'I UNDERSTAND that you wanted to speak to me?'

It would have been wiser for him to accede to Ionanthe's formal request to his aide by seeing her somewhere other than in this bedroom. All the more so when he had spent the last eight nights avoiding coming anywhere near it—because he couldn't trust his own self-control to prevent him from reacting to the danger-ous mix of fierce anger and equally fierce sexual desire she aroused in him, Max recognized. But it was too late for him to regret that error now. He could hardly have ignored it, after all—not when she had delivered it so very publicly, via his *aide de camp*.

What did she want? he wondered. Money? Jewellery? Her sister had asked for both those things and more. He thought angrily of the obvious and pitiful poverty of that group of men who had been prepared to risk their lives, if necessary, for the sake of Ionanthe's honour.

'Yes,' Ionanthe confirmed. She couldn't bring herself to look at Max. She didn't trust herself to do so. They had been married for just over a week—eight days, in fact, and eight long, humiliating nights. All of which she had spent alone in a bed that was obviously designed to accommodate two people—the bed that she was determined not to look at now, even though its presence in the room dominated her thoughts almost as much as Max's absence from it had dominated them during these last eight days of a marriage that was in effect no marriage at all.

Because she was not her sister? The pain of her childhood, with its lack of love and her grandfather's rejection, must not be allowed to affect her now. She must not allow herself to appear vulnerable or needy. She must demand what was her right—not for her own sake, of course. She had no desire to share the intimacy of sex with a man who, having forced her into marriage, now chose to ignore her. After all, she had never been the kind of woman who was driven by her own sexual need—far from it. In fact, going without sex had, if anything, become her preferred way of life, and one she had been happy with. No. It was for the sake of the people that she was forcing herself to put aside her own personal feelings. Alone, she could not change things for them. She knew that. The island's society was one rooted in the past, in which the male head of the family held absolute control. It would take a man to change that—a very strong, very aware, very courageous man. A son. *Her* son. A man who would be enlightened enough to change things for his people.

Despite her own lack of any need to be a sexually desired woman, there was still the undeniable fact that Max's very public rejection of her had left her feeling humiliated. Theirs was not, after all, a 'normal' marriage. As the island's ruler Max had to live very much in the public eye, and as his wife so did she. It would have been easy enough to bear if only *she* had known about her husband's sexual rejection of her, but of course the rest of the court was bound to know. Ionanthe hadn't missed the sympathetic looks her maid had been giving her every morning for the last eight mornings. The fact that everyone knew that Max had married her because he needed a son, and yet had not consummated their marriage shamed and insulted her, turning her into a laughing stock. She was not prepared to tolerate the situation any longer.

Max could feel his muscles, in fact his whole body, tensing against Ionanthe's presence, whilst at the same time his senses strained to absorb as much of it and her as they could. The room smelled of her, of the scent she always wore, which somehow he had learned to search for in the rooms from which she herself was absent. In the long, aching reaches of the empty nights it had tormented him, conjuring up for him images of it cloaking her skin and scenting the darkness until he'd felt he was being driven close to madness by the folly of his own savage hunger for her. How had it come to this? How was it possible for him to want her so deeply and so compulsively?

Max didn't have the answer to that question. The manner in which his physical hunger for her suspended all that was rational and normal for him was something he couldn't analyse to any satisfactory conclusion. Not that he hadn't tried; he had. And in the end all he'd been able to tell himself was that the desire that burned inside him was simply the result of some primitive male instinct within himself that had been unleashed by her behaviour towards him.

He had been with his personal aide, the son of one of the island's barons when Ionanthe's lady-in-waiting had brought the message that Ionanthe wished to speak with him, so it had been impossible for him to ignore it.

Ionanthe took a deep breath and, still keeping her back to the bed, began. 'Your absence from our marital bed has humiliated me and made me the subject of court gossip.'

Max fought to control his body's reaction to her words. Only he knew how hard it had been for him to keep to his decision not to give in to his growing desire for her. He would not partner her in the kind of cold and clinical intercourse she had described to him as the manner in which she wished to consummate their marriage. He would not, or did he fear that he *could* not? Max was forced to ask himself. Wasn't it true that he was staying away from the bed they should have shared because he was afraid that if he did share it with her he would not be able to control the desire she aroused in him? The fact that she should arouse that desire was difficult enough for him to come to terms with, without having to add his concern that he would not be able to control it. It had, after all, come out of nowhere, with such speed and power that it had left him punch-drunk, reeling and, worst of all, feeling that he could no longer trust his own carefully set inner controls. No woman had ever affected him as Ionanthe did. No woman had ever aroused him to such a pitch of aching need combined with furious anger—

severing him from the man he had always thought himself to be when it came to sexual needs. That man had been willing to follow his partner's wishes, been very careful to keep the emotional temperature on merely warm. That man had certainly never had to deal with the kind of raw, demanding need he was experiencing now.

Why? He had barely registered the fact that Ionanthe even existed before he had met her, and yet now here he was…

Here he was *what*? Here he was wanting her so desperately and so passionately that he barely recognised himself any more?

Max's mouth hardened—the only outwardly visible sign of his inner demons and one that Ionanthe registered as antagonism towards her.

Max was trying to force her to back down. Well, she wasn't going to.

The proud arching of her neck as she lifted her chin to confront him brought a sharp shock of physical reaction to Max's senses. He wanted to cover the distance between them—to cover *her* in the most basic and intimate way. He wanted to slide his hand and then his mouth down the tormenting oh-so-proud and yet vulnerable arch of her creamy-fleshed neck. He wanted to pushed aside the neat fawn cashmere sweater she was wearing and explore the curve of her shoulder, tasting her, knowing her, feeling her breast swell into his hand and her nipple harden and tighten in his palm.

Oblivious to Max's reaction to her, Ionanthe pressed on.

'Either you bring that humiliation to an end by consummating our marriage,' she told him determinedly, ' or…'

Her words were like the worst kind of sharp blows against already dangerously raw and open wounds, overloading his self-control, inflaming him, driving him into an unfamiliar place where the red mist that came down over him obliterated everything else, Max acknowledged. All he could think, all he knew, was that she was tormenting him to the point where he had to put some distance between them or risk them both facing the consequences.

'This isn't a discussion I want to pursue,' he told her flatly, turning his back on her and heading for the door.

For a second Ionanthe was too frozen with anger and disbelief to say or do anything. But then desperation drove her, and she ran for the door, reaching it ahead of Max and flattening her back against it, her arms outspread as she told him fiercely, 'That's not good enough. I won't be treated like that. I want an answer from you, and I am not going to let you leave this room until I get one.'

Max was so close to her that he could feel the sweet warmth of her breath against his skin. He wanted to close his eyes to blot out her image, but he couldn't. How ironic it was that, whilst all Ionanthe wanted from him was a clinical and detached act of consummation, her sister had actively wanted to reduce him to wanting her, with all her wiles and coquettish well-used tricks. But she had never once come anywhere near arousing him to one tenth of the desire rampaging through him right now—for Ionanthe. A desire he had to control.

'Stand aside,' he commanded Ionanthe, stepping up to her and reaching out to grasp the handle of the door.

'No,' Ionanthe refused.

Her denial was all the spark the dry tinderbox of tensions within him needed. Max's self-control snapped. With one swift movement he imprisoned her against the door, the hand he had previously curled round the door handle now gripping her hip, whilst his other hand pinioned her shoulder.

'You want an answer? Very well then—let *this* be your answer,' Max told her, crushing his mouth down on hers, imprinting the shape and taste of it on her lips just as the weight of his body was imprinting itself against her flesh, forcing her to accept his domination.

This wasn't what she had wanted—so why was she allowing him to impose the bruising pressure of his kiss on her? How had she moved so quickly from holding the high ground with justifiable anger to this place where she was now, where her whole body was awash with a flood of sensations she didn't want and *he* was the one in control?

Somehow she managed to break the kiss, straining back from him, her heart racing from the exertion—the exertion or the excitement? The exertion, of course. He didn't excite her. How could he? She tried to pull away from him, and for a second, as his hands lifted from her body, she thought she had succeeded. But he didn't let her get very far.

His hands closed on her shoulders as he swung her round, so that he was the one leaning on the door and somehow or other she was leaning on him—on him and into him—her whole body pressed into his, making her aware of her own flesh and its sexuality in a way that shocked through her like lightning. Why had she never known before that the pressure of a man's hard muscular chest against her breasts could turn their rounded softness into a mass of sensually receptive nerve-endings? Or that the pump of a male heartbeat lifting its owner's chest against her could translate into something that her breasts interpreted as a caress, and to which they responded with a fierce ache that tore at her flesh?

That ache sent images into her head that were visually and sensually erotic—images of Max's dark head bent over her naked body, his lips capturing the flaunting demand of her puckered nipples and drawing on them until her pleasure reached a crescendo that made her want to moan out loud—she could hardly believe that she was experiencing them.

But she was. And she was experiencing too the heavy low drag of need that was filling her lower body as it rested against his, making her want to press closer to him, making her want to grind her hips eagerly against him, making her *want*. A shudder of wild delight gripped her when Max's hands slid down to her hips, pulling her even more intimately against him whilst his lips pillaged the vulnerable flesh of her throat.

Something unfamiliar and dangerous slid through her veins, like a heady, intoxicating potion that stripped her of her will to deal in the factual and logical. It carried her with it on a tide that reacted to Max's maleness with the same kind of magnetic pull that the moon had on the oceans of the world.

He should have stopped before this, Max knew,

whilst he had still been able to stop. Now it was too late. He swept Ionanthe up into his arms and carried her towards the bed.

As he placed her on it Ionanthe tried to listen to the inner voice warning her that she was in danger—tried to draw back from him as he started to undress her.

'You were the one who wanted this,' Max reminded her as he leaned over her, removed her skirt and then her sweater.

'Not like this,' Ionanthe protested.

Not like *what*?

He was kissing her again, nuzzling her throat, stringing kisses against it so delicate and yet so sensual that they dizzied her senses and robbed her of any ability to verbalise her true feelings. Instead she was arching her throat, offering it up to him and then shuddering in mute pleasure when the heat of his mouth became more possessive.

His hands on her bra had somehow become an aid, an ally, understanding her need to be clothed only by his touch. But Max seemed more disposed to linger over the silky underwear that was her one concession to the demands of her femininity rather than remove it speedily. Her frustration grew.

Through the fine silk of her underwear Max could see the dark thrust of Ionanthe's nipples, and the even darker softness of the hair covering her sex. She dressed so primly on the outside that to see her clothed in such a way underneath was somehow unbearably erotic. Was it possible that her outwardly cold manner could conceal a passionate heat? Desire kicked fiercely through him at the thought of her meeting and matching him in the white-hot conflagration of shared need. He kissed the exposed upper slope of her breast, savouring the sweetness of her flesh, slowly easing away the silk until he could stroke his tongue-tip against her nipple.

Ionanthe cried out sharply, the sound torn from her in response to the shockingly intense stab of pleasure that pierced her, lifting her from the bed to arch against Max's mouth. Her hand rose to cup the back of his head, her fingers curling into the thickness of his hair as she gave herself up to the hot pleasure his mouth was spilling through her. In response his hand covered her sex, probing the barrier of fragile silk and lace that was no barrier at all, slipping beyond it to find the warm wetness that waited for him.

The late afternoon light slipped away into darkness without Ionanthe being aware of the passage of time. She was capable only of measuring time by the acceleration of the growing ache of need that had possessed her. The whole purpose of her life, what she had been born for, had become distilled into this concentration of her entire being, so that it could be given up to the moment that would create life even while everything she had thought she was fell away and burned, dying in the conflagration of creating that spark of new life.

These thoughts and many others whirled inside her head kaleidoscope-like, meaning nothing. Her thoughts were incapable of doing anything to bring to a halt what she herself had set in motion, and nor did she want them to.

But this was not a time for thinking. It was a time for feeling, for knowing, for believing, for giving herself up to the sensation of Max's hands and lips on her body. Every part of her pulsated with the urge for completion that was driving her. Every nerve-ending within her was so sensitised to and by his caresses that she felt that he could take her no higher, that the moment of culmination was there, a mere tantalising half a breath out of reach.

But Max would not allow her that culmination. By some alchemic force and power surely only he alone possessed he drew the fine skein of thread linking her to her desire higher and tighter, to her gasped litany of pleas and protests. Ignoring her plea to him not to torment her any further, he continued to prove to her that she was wrong and that he could. With the deliberate and lingering stroke of his tongue-tip against the pulsing thrust of flesh that was her sex and the intimate caress of his fingers within her he brought her time and time again to the point where the release she wanted was within reach—only to change his caresses to a gentler pace, brushing butterfly wing kisses against her inner thighs whilst he stroked the soft flesh there, keeping her at an unbearable pitch of need whilst refusing to satisfy it.

He couldn't hold out much longer, Max acknowledged as he tried to separate his body from his mind and ignore the furious clamour and the almost physical pain of his self-denial. He ached with every cell he possessed to slide himself fully and deeply into the warm eager wetness Ionanthe was so eagerly offering him and take them both to orgasm. But he couldn't; not yet. Not until he was sure she was ready to give him what he had to have.

The winter sunlight had long ago given way to the silvery light of the rising moon, painting Ionanthe's body in silver and charcoal. She would make a magnificent subject for an artist's eye, he thought. Her hair a dark tumbling mass around her shoulders, the bone structure beneath her skin delineated by the stardust silver brush on her shoulder, her hip, her thigh, whilst her flesh itself was moonlight-pale, her nipples charcoal-rose and the secret places of her body an inviting velvety night-sky-dark.

He wanted to lose himself completely with her and within her. No woman had ever made him feel like this, want like this, need like this—but no other woman had made him question her purpose and her beliefs either. Because no other woman had been important enough for him to *have* such feelings.

The sensual intimacy he was using against Ionanthe was a two-edged sword, Max recognised. He might be breaking down her contemptuous claim that for her sex between them could only be a cold, clinical matter, but in doing so he was creating within himself an emotional awareness of her, a closeness to her that could run totally counter to his determination to put his people and their needs before anything else.

He was creating problems where none needed to exist, Max told himself. This was a one-off—a response to the challenge Ionanthe had thrown at him.

He bent his head and painted slow, sensual circles of erotic delight on Ionanthe's inner thigh, drawing the thread of her desire even tighter. Helpless to stop herself, Ionanthe reached down between her parted thighs to cup the back of Max's head, unable to tell whether she wanted to keep him where he was or urge him to return and repeat the earlier, previously unknown intimacy he had shown her. She knew only that she could not bear it if he withdrew from her.

But he did, lifting his head to look at her through the moonlit darkness to demand softly, 'So tell me now, Ionanthe, whilst you are still capable of saying the words and I am rational enough to hear them, how do you *really* prefer your sex? Cold and clinical? Or like this? Which is best?'

His touch stroked slowly, warmly, wetly the length of her, and then rested firmly against her clitoris before once more he lifted his head for her answer.

He hadn't said that this would be the end—an end that would be no end at all since it would leave her gripped by agonising need—but the fear that that was what he had in mind was enough for her body to command her brain.

'*This* is best,' she admitted, closing her eyes as her body forced aside her pride, making her lips form words she had never thought she would utter. '*You* are the best,' she added helplessly. "I have nev—' She gasped and cried out—a low, guttural sound of aching pleasure as Max responded to her initial admission with the slow, powerful, deep thrust of his body within her own.

How could something so primitive, so basic, designed by nature and not the human mind, meet so perfectly the needs of flesh and the senses? Ionanthe wondered dizzily, instinctively tightening her muscles around the slick, hot male flesh that was not just filling her but stroking into her, receiving back from her a growing urgency. But then whilst nature might have provided the ingredients for her pleasure, it was Max who had taken them and honed them.

The climb grew steeper, making demands on her she had never known existed. Ionanthe fought for breath, for the strength to endure—and for purchase, so as not to lose her place on the sharp incline.

The summit was there, within reach—so dazzlingly beautiful, so immortal, so achingly needed that its promise brought the sting of tears to her eyes. And somehow he knew, even through his own journey. Just for a beat of time she wavered, half afraid of reaching the pinnacle, knowing that once she did she must fling herself headlong into its glory and give up all her sense of self. And then Max was there, whispering to her. 'Now…' His hand reached for hers, his fingers entwining with her hers, holding her safe as the moment came and together they defied time and mortality. Together…

As the force of the moment shook her body, the knowledge burned into Ionanthe's spirit that in those final seconds, with the peak so close and yet not reached, all she had wanted—all she had ached and yearned for— was to reach it with Max. Not one thought had she had for the son for whom she had married Max and begun the journey they had just completed. Not one thought had she given to the people. Her sacrifice of self had not been for them but instead for the need that had burned in her for the man who was now holding her.

'Max?'

The sound of his name, spoken in a voice drenched with a heart-aching mix of emotions, had Max drawing Ionanthe closer to him, covering her body with the protective warmth and strength of his own in the same way that he suddenly longed to cloak her emotions and keep her from pain. He had driven her hard, fuelled by anger to punish her for the damage she had done to his pride, but now, rather than flaunt his triumph to her, he wanted instead to protect her.

As he held her Max felt Ionanthe slip into sleep, her breathing becoming even and soft against his skin. Very carefully and gently he detached himself from her, stilling when in her sleep she frowned, as though reluctant to let him go. He continued when she didn't wake. There were things he had to do, duties he had to perform, responsibilities he could not and should not evade.

CHAPTER SIX

SOMETHING sweetly juicy was moistening her dry lips, causing her to part them the better to taste it. The pleasurable sensation woke Ionanthe from her sleep.

Fresh peach! A luxury in December, and grown, she remembered, in the hothouses of the summer palace, built in the eighteenth century on the site where centuries before the Moorish rulers of the island had also taken advantage of the most southerly facing coastline of Fortenegro to cultivate dates and grow peaches.

A more concerned and less selfish ruler would have used that fertile and protected land for the good of his people, rather than himself, ordering that the land be turned over to the production of fruit and vegetables for the export markets of Northern Europe. It was equally selfish of her to enjoy the taste of something grown only for the pleasure of one selfish man. But her mouth was dry, and the scent of the fruit as well as its taste was tormenting her senses. Slowly, Ionanthe opened her eyes.

Beyond the windows the sky was still night-dark, but now in the room beyond the bedroom a fire burned in the modern central fireplace, throwing out from its flames soft colour and warmth.

It was Max who was tempting her, his skin tanned against the whiteness of the towelling robe he was wearing, his feet bare—as he would be beneath his robe. A huge lump formed in her throat. She reached up to push away his hand, chagrin charging her emotions. But Max was ready for her rejection, his free hand firmly cupping the side of her face.

'You should eat.'

The words were calm enough, but something her body heard in them that her ears could not sent a stab of something primitive and shamefully sweet kicking through her, and this time when he offered her the fruit her fingers rested on his wrist, as though she feared he might withdraw before she could bite into the slice of juicy peach.

Its taste was heavenly, sharply sweet, quenching her thirst.

'More?' Max asked softly.

Again her body responded ahead of her mind—her breath quickening, her gaze sleepily possessive as it fastened on his lips, watching him speak to her. Her assent might only have been a brief nod of her head, but it was enough. More than enough, she recognized, when Max held out to her the cream silk peignoir she had bought on impulse in Paris whilst waiting for her connecting flight to the island. Little had she known then just where and how she would be wearing it.

Ionanthe trembled a little as she turned her back on him to slip her arms into its sleeves. She had had to step from the bed naked, and she had been aware when she did so of the unashamed and intent way in which he had openly absorbed her nakedness. Now, with the warmth of that watchful caress still upon her, she trembled slightly. Because of the way he had looked at her, or because of her own secret but equally unashamed deep-rooted enjoyment of that visual caress from a sexually triumphant man in possession?

Out of nowhere a new road had been carved through the once impenetrable barriers of her mind, allowing her access to places within herself she didn't really want to go. It was easier to focus on other things—such as the fact that Max had obviously been busy whilst she had slept, as evidenced by the lit fire and the small banquet she could now see laid out on low tables within reach of the sitting room's luxuriously comfortable and deeply upholstered sofas. She could see fruit from the royal succession houses—peach, fig, nectarines—and almond sweets dusted with sugar—an Island speciality like the delicately flavoured local goats cheese, roasted and mixed with salad, served with seeded flat unleavened local bread and island-grown olives. There was even a bottle of the island's wine, although it was a glass of champagne that Max now poured for her.

Her sister's favourite drink. Her hand trembled, her heart chilling.

Max watched Ionanthe, trying to hold on to his resolution. He had chosen their food deliberately, focusing on what the island produced in an attempt to remind himself of his duty instead of giving way to his personal need.

Only now, in the aftermath of their shared passion,

was the true legacy of what he had done hitting him. He had allowed his pride and his anger to push him into ignoring the warnings he had already registered, which he *should* have listened to. Warnings such as the unexpectedly powerful effect Ionanthe had had on his senses at their first meeting. Warnings regarding his increasing awareness of his desire for her. Warnings which had urged him to recognise that it would be fatally easy to step off the path he had chosen for himself. Because—most dangerous of all—it wasn't merely physically that she affected him.

Was she aware that the small banquet in front of her comprised food and drink that came from the island but which was available only to the very wealthy? This kind of food and drink could and should provide not only a better diet for the people of the island but could also be exported, to provide them with a better income and bring in money which could be invested to the benefit of everyone—helping to pay for an improved infrastructure, for schools and hospitals and ultimately, through them, bringing better jobs for people and brighter futures. Or was she oblivious to all of that? Unknowing and uncaring?

Even worse, was she, as her sister had been, not just oblivious to but actively *against* the plans he had to persuade those who held most of the island's fertile land by virtue of nothing more than inherited titles to allow it to be let out at a peppercorn rent for the benefit of the people? He planned to do so with much of the land he himself as Prince now owned. But her grandfather, after all, had been the most antagonistic of all his courtiers, and Max had swiftly come to recognise that the Baron's plan to marry his granddaughter to him had not just been to secure for her the highest status in the island but, more ambitiously, because he had hoped to influence and if possible rule the island from behind the throne.

Max could still remember the quarrel between them after he had told Eloise that he would not take her to South of France to attend a celebrity party because he had set up a meeting with some Spanish growers whose advice he wanted to seek. She had announced with semi-drunken spite that he was a fool, and that her grandfather would never allow him to put his plans into practice.

He had known then that their marriage was dead. The revulsion with which Eloise had filled him had ensured that.

And Ionanthe was her sister. Brought up by the same man and in the same manner. He must not forget that.

He waited for her to take the glass of champagne he had poured for her, but Ionanthe shook her head.

'Some, wine, then?' he offered. 'Although I should warn you that it is strong and…'

'You should warn me?' Ionanthe stopped him. 'You seem to be forgetting that I grew up here—that I am perfectly well aware of the strength of our home-grown wine.' As she spoke Ionanthe reached for the bottle and poured herself a glass. She would rather have drunk poison, she told herself bitterly, than to drink her sister's beloved bubbly.

The truth was that she rarely drank alcohol at all, but she wasn't going to tell him that. Lifting her glass to her lips, she took a deep swallow. The firelight on the glass warmed the potent darkness of its contents, just as the wine itself was now warming her, spreading a heat that relaxed the angry tension that had been clutching tight fingers round her heart.

She drank some more, grateful for the wine's immediate and empowering effect on her senses. And then she made the mistake of looking directly at Max, and immediately that empowerment transformed itself into a dizzying and weakening surge of female awareness of his maleness, heightened by her body's memory of the pleasure he had already shown it.

Could two gulps of wine be enough to make her feel like this? Far more likely her blood sugar level had plunged and she needed something to eat, Ionanthe reassured herself, turning abruptly towards the table. Embarrassingly, she almost stumbled, so that Max had to step forward and take hold of her.

Wide-eyed, she looked up at him. Why was it that the expensive fabric of her peignoir suddenly felt oppressive? Its touch was making her nipples feel so acutely sensitive that she wanted to pull it off. Why was it, too, that her heart was thudding so heavily and so unsteadily?

Steadying her with one hand, Max removed the wine glass from her hold with the other, putting it down and then telling her, 'I think you should sit down, don't you?' He guided her towards the sofa.

No, Ionanthe thought rebelliously as he calmly but firmly urged her onto the sofa. What I should do is go back to bed, so that you can do everything you did before all over again.

Shock spiralled through her. Was she really having such alien thoughts? Where had they come from?

Max watched her with a small frown. She'd hardly touched the wine and yet her cheeks were flushed, her eyes brilliant, her lips swollen with promise.

His groin began to ache. His frown deepened. More sex wasn't what he had had in mind when he had ordered this intimate supper and instructed the staff to leave them alone. What he had wanted to do was find out what basis they might have for beginning a relationship that might work.

He reached for the plate of figs that was close to his hand, intending only to ensure that Ionanthe had something to eat. But when he offered the plate to her she used her free hand to hold his wrist as she took one, so that he could not put the plate down or step back from her without pushing her away.

Her gaze on his, she bit into the fruit, causing its dusting of powdered sugar to cling to her lips and fall to her body, speckling the flesh exposed by the opening of her robe.

The fig was sweet and sticky. When she had finished eating it Ionanthe looked round for a napkin, and then put one of her fingers in her mouth and licked it.

Max felt reaction implode inside him, wiring his whole body to immediate fierce desire. He put down the plate and reached for Ionanthe's arm, taking the sticky fingers one by one into his own mouth and sucking slowly on them.

Ionanthe drew in her breath and then exhaled it on a small sob of physical delight, silenced when Max released her hand to kiss the sweetness from her mouth. When she wanted to demand something more intimate he used his tongue to lick the sugar from her skin at the V her robe exposed—the tantalisingly small area of flesh where her breasts started to rise from the valley between them. Her nipples pressed eagerly against her peignoir, the agitation of her breathing increasing the silk's movement against them so that the delicate friction became a torment of aroused sensitivity. Wild thoughts flashed though her head, filling her with reckless excitement.

She pushed Max away, giving him a small secret smile when he obeyed, but looked as though he had done so with reluctance. She reached for the plate Max had put down and then, balancing it on her lap, unfastened her wrap and shrugged her arms free of it. It slipped down to pool round her waist, leaving the top half of her body to be clothed only by firelight. Then, watching Max as she did so, she picked up one of the figs and began to eat it, very slowly, whilst its sugar coating drifted down onto her naked breasts.

Liquid fire ran through Max's veins. Ionanthe's playful sensuality intoxicated him far more than any amount of alcohol might have done. Had she somehow *known* what was going on inside his head earlier, when he had licked the sugar from her skin? Had she read his mind and guessed then that mentally he was visualising her exactly as she was now? No, not *exactly* as she was now, he admitted. His imagination had not had the power to do her full justice. It had not, for instance, painted her nipples with such dark swollen crowns that the sugar speckling them made him want not merely to lick it from them but to taste them and suck them.

Ionanthe watched Max with the liquid-dark secret knowledge of a woman. The kind of knowledge that came not just from knowing a man in the most intimate physical way there was, but also from seeing the pure essence of him laid bare through the power of mutual desire and need. Without having to question or doubt Ionanthe knew beyond mere ordinary knowing that the desire running through her, the images inside her head, the need driving her, were all things that were in their different ways reflections of what Max himself was experiencing.

When he came to her without haste, his desire so charged that she could feel its heat burning her own skin, she was ready for him. There was no need for any words between them. She bit deeply into the small fruit he was holding out to her, and then offered him the unbitten half, keeping his gaze even when his fingers gripped her wrist and his lips brushed her fingertips as he took the fruit from her hold.

Without words to accompany them, somehow the symbolic gestures they were sharing took on an almost sacred intimacy—as though in some way they were enacting a ritual that went all the way back into the mists of human time, as though the blood of the ancestry they shared mingled with their own to move powerfully and quicken within them, taking them to heights that for Ionanthe would have been unimaginable twenty-four hours beforehand.

As the firelight played and glistened on their desire-drenched bodies they came together, to ascend the peak and then to freefall from it into infinity—not just once, but throughout all the night hours as the desire within them rose higher to new heights by way of new pleasures.

And not once, as her body strained for pleasure and release, did Ionanthe think of the son she had sworn to herself was the only purpose for her being here.

The morning came slowly and kindly, waking Max first, so that he had the pleasure of watching Ionanthe whilst she slept, her body resting against his, her skin smelling of the musky intimacy of the night and of *her*, the heady combination sending a slow wave of freshly burgeoning desire uncurling within him.

Whilst he watched her Ionanthe's eyes opened. Perhaps mystically she had sensed his need, as though it had called out to her, bringing her from the depths of sleep. Max derided himself inwardly for the danger of such thoughts. It was simply because he had moved that he had woken her. Nothing more. And yet without a word Ionanthe leaned over him, seeking his lips with her own, her hand sliding down his naked body until she reached the rigid swell of his penis.

Her kiss deepened, and her swift movement to straddle him surprised and delighted him. His hands immediately went to her hips to assist her as he lifted her onto his erection.

Max's eyes closed in mute pleasure as she took him slowly into her body, tormenting him a little with the soft caress of her muscles. And then, just when he thought the torment would be too much for him, Ionanthe began to rise and fall on him, slowly at first, taking him deeper and deeper within herself, holding him there, and then faster—until he was the one holding her down onto him, and she was the one crying out the ache of her need and the glory of its fulfilment.

Afterwards they showered together—Max quickly, leaving Ionanthe alone to enjoy the warmth of the water.

When she returned to the bedroom she saw that he had made a small breakfast for them of tea and toast.

'Of course if you'd also like some fruit…' Max teased her, but Ionanthe shook her head even whilst the colour bloomed in her face.

She felt too languid to quarrel with him. Too… Too satisfied? Her face burned hotter.

CHAPTER SEVEN

IT WAS six hours and ten minutes since she had woken up alone in bed to the realisation of what she had done. And it was over eight hours since she had last seen Max—longer since they had last…

Ionanthe made an agitated turn of the floor of their private sitting room. What she had done, the way she had behaved, was unforgivable, unacceptable, unbearable. The more she relived the events of the night the more she hated and despised herself. It was impossible now for her to cling to the excuse that her behaviour had been caused by her desire to conceive a son—a future ruler for the people. The truth was that there had been no thought of him in her head or driving her body when she had hungered over and over again for Max's possession.

What was the cause of her behaviour, then? Too many years of celibacy? Too many years of low sexual self-esteem after living in the shadow of her sister? If she was going to go down that track then why not shift the blame from herself altogether? Ionanthe derided herself. Why not blame the wine, or the figs, or—? She stood completely still, not even drawing breath. Or why not blame the one who had conjured desire from her flesh—the man who had put her under his spell and who had brought from her the need that had overwhelmed her? It was easier, surely, to blame Max—who, after all, had been the one to start the conflagration that had destroyed everything she had previously thought about her own sexuality—than to accept the sharply painful suggestion that she might have been the authoress of her own downfall.

As she struggled to battle with her responsibility for protecting herself and her responsibility to acknowledge the truth, unconnected, barely formed, but still very distracting thoughts weaved themselves though her pain. Thoughts such as how she would never, ever forget the scent of Max's flesh, pre-arousal, during it, and in its final culmination. Such as how there had been a certain look in his eyes, a certain tension in his body that her senses would forever recognize. Thoughts such as how could her sister have wanted to have sex with other men when she'd had Max—a man, a husband, so able to satisfy her every sexual need?

Had he held Eloise as he had held her? Had he touched her? Aroused her? Satisfied her?

Pain ripped through her, savaging her, stripping back the protective layer of her emotional skin to leave its nerve-endings exposed and raw.

Dear God, what was she doing to herself? Hadn't she caused herself enough harm already without adding more? Right now, in order to protect herself, she must not think about what had happened. Instead she must summon all her mental powers and somehow ignore it.

Why not demand that her brain go one step further and attempt to convince herself that it had never happened at all? Ionanthe derided herself. Why not simply pretend that last night had never been?

By rights she ought to have the courage to face up to what had happened. Was she a woman capable of producing and guiding the boy who would become the man who would stand tall and strong for the causes of right and justice for the weak and poor? Or was she simply a coward?

This wasn't a contest between bravery and cowardice, Ionanthe told herself. It was instead a matter of survival—of living with the weakness and the vulnerability she had found within herself whilst continuing to pursue her objectives. And that could start right now, with her making sure that Max understood that what had happened last night had been a one-off. After all, even though shamefully she had not thought of it last night, she might already have conceived her son. It would take time for her to know, of course, but until she did there was no reason for her to continue to have sex with Max, was there? She had been weak, but here was her chance to regain the self-respect she had lost. All she had to do was convey her decision to Max.

And when and where would she do that? In his arms? In bed? In the silvery moonlight with his hands on her body? While he knew her and possessed her so intimately and completely that they were almost as one?

A deep shudder wrenched at her body.

'And then there is the matter of the consortium wishing to apply for permission to excavate a coal mine on Your

Highness's land. You will remember that I informed you that your late cousin was on the point of granting them a licence just before his death?'

Max frowned as he listened to the Count. 'As I remember, that land is usually let out to—'

'Sheep farmers. Yes. But there is no formal agreement. You have the right to move their stock off the land if you wish to do so.'

Max's frown deepened. He was keen to invest in renewable energy sources for the island, but these plans were still in their infancy and he was not yet ready to go public with them or discuss them with the Count.

'I am due to fly to Spain tomorrow,' he pointed out instead.

'Indeed? Shall the Princess be accompanying you?'

The Count's question was, on the face of it, justified. But Max still gave him a sharp look. He was rewarded when the other man continued smoothly, 'If I may be permitted to say so, Your Highness, I am delighted to see that things are working out so well between you. Had I been consulted in the first place, I would have suggested then that if you were determined to marry one of the late Baron's granddaughters then his younger granddaughter would be by far the better choice. Whilst Ionanthe may never have found favour in her late grandfather's eyes, it was always obvious to those with the wit to see it that she far outshone her sister. As a child Ionanthe was always the one who felt more passionately about the island and its people. It was a source of great sorrow to her parents, I know, that she was not born a son. For then the traditions of their family—a family that has always upheld the way of life of our island—would have been assured. But Ionanthe will make you an excellent consort. She is well versed in our ways.'

The Count sounded as pleased with himself—as though he himself had created Ionanthe.

Max gave him a sharp look. It was, of course, impossible to keep anything hidden from the members of a court who virtually lived together. Everyone would know by now that he and Ionanthe had spent the night together, and would have drawn their own conclusions from that. Was the Count hoping that through Ionanthe pressure could be brought to bear on him to accept their way of life rather than insist on changing it? It had, after all, been the Count who had been so instrumental in forcing this marriage on them. On them, or on *him*?

Half an hour later, alone in the Chamber of State, Max reminded himself that he had warned himself all along of the dangers inherent in becoming intimately and emotionally involved with Ionanthe. Now was the time to take a step back, to remember the reason why he was here, playing a feudal role in an equally feudal country that was surely more akin to a Gilbert and Sullivan creation than part of the modern world.

And what of Ionanthe's own beliefs? Max had no need of anyone to tell him that Ionanthe's sexual and moral code was a world away from that of her sister, or that she was one of life's givers rather than one of its takers. But, as he had already discovered, those who by their own decree had long held the right to high office on the island felt passionately about the traditions they upheld, and were passionate in their refusal to allow any change. And Ionanthe was a very passionate woman.

He might not need her support to put in place the changes he planned to make, but neither did he intend to put himself in a position where he was afraid that confidences he let slip to Ionanthe in the intimacy of their bed might be passed on to those who opposed his plans.

It was perhaps as well that he was flying to Barcelona tomorrow.

Tonight would be different; tonight she would not give way or weaken. Tonight she would be the woman, the Ionanthe, she had to be from now on, she had assured herself as she had dressed for the formal dinner that was being held tonight for Philippe de la Croix, a French diplomat who was visiting from Paris.

But that had been before she had seen Max—before he had thrust open the door to their private quarters and come striding towards her, causing her heart to slam into her ribs and her whole body to go weak.

The pleasure he had shown her was not hers alone, she tried to remind herself. He had been married to her sister, after all—a woman who had been far more sexually experienced and desirable than she was herself. The savagery of the pain coiling through her shocked her. So this was jealousy, red-hot and raw, filling her with a fierce, possessive need to obliterate the memory of her sister from his mind and his senses, shaming her with its primitive message. She tried to block the destructive thoughts from her mind, but still they went on forcing themselves onto her, burning her where they touched her vulnerable places.

Today, studying the cooling ashes of last night's passion, had he compared her to Eloise and found her wanting? *Aaahhh,* but that hurt so very much, reducing the pain of the rejection she had known as a child to nothing—a shadow of this so much greater agony. Was it because she had known all along that she would feel like this that she had fought so hard against loving a man?

Loving a man? But she did not *love* Max. She could not. It was impossible. She barely knew him.

She knew enough of him to know his touch and its effect on her senses. He had marked her indelibly as his, and nothing could change that. If that was not a form of loving then— No. She would not allow it to be. It must not be. She must escape from what was happening to her, from him.

She took a deep breath and announced shakily, 'I should like your permission to withdraw to my family's estate. There are matters there that need my attention following my grandfather's death, and if I delay going there much longer the castle will be cut off by the winter snows.'

In truth Ionanthe knew that there was not likely to be any real need for her to visit the castle. Her grandfather had disliked it because of its isolation, and had rarely gone there after the death of her parents, preferring to base himself here, in his State apartment. Eloise had loathed the castle, and had always treated the simple country people who lived close to it, working manually on the estate as their families had done for many generations, with acid contempt.

Their parents, though, *had* spent time there—her mother encouraging Ionanthe when she had tried to teach the young children of the estate workers to read. Those had been happy days—until her grandfather had found out about her impromptu classes and roared at her in anger, telling her mother that she was not to encourage the 'labourers' brats' to waste their time on learning skills they did not need.

That had been when Ionanthe had recognised that even her parents were not strong enough to stand up to her grandfather.

Max listened to her in silence. He did not for one minute believe that she really felt any urgent desire to visit the remote castle she had inherited from her grandfather. He suspected, in fact, that the real reason for her request was a desire on her part to distance herself from last night. But he was not going to challenge her on that point. Why should he, when it suited him so well? And yet there was a feeling within him of antagonism towards her announcement—a latent need to assert the right that his body felt last night had given it to keep her close, a surge of male hostility at her desire to separate herself from him.

All merely primitive male ego drives that must be ignored, Max told himself firmly. And to prove that he intended to do exactly that, he nodded his head and told Ionanthe calmly, 'Of course you may have my permission.'

Her relief was immediate, and visible in the exhalation of her breath. Was it her relief that speared him, conjuring up his swift response?

'There is, after all, no reason for me to withhold it. I trust that you are thoroughly satisfied now that we have consummated our marriage?' He gave emphasis to the word 'satisfied' rather than the far less dangerous and emotive 'now' that followed.

Was this man now deliberately tormenting her the same man who only last night had fed her—fed on the desire he had created within her? She ought to despise him, not be in danger of loving him, Ionanthe told herself angrily.

'I am satisfied that I have performed my duty.' It was all she could think of to say in response.

'Duty—such a cold word, and so wholly inappropriate for—'

To Ionanthe's relief, before Max could finish delivering his intended taunt someone had knocked on the door, bringing their conversation to a halt and allowing her to escape to prepare herself for the evening's formal dinner.

If growing up observing her grandfather's Machiavellian attitude to court politics had taught Ionanthe a great deal about how the world of wealth and power operated, and in addition given her a private antipathy towards it, then her working life in Brussels had given her an inner resilience, equipped her to deal with it whilst keeping her own private counsel. She knew the rules of engagement that governed the subtle wars of status and power that underwrote policy and the way it was managed: via a tightly woven mesh of lobbyists, business interests, law-makers and law-breakers. As a child, witnessing the court of Fortenegro's crushing need for power as evidenced by her grandfather had hurt her. But now, returning to the island as a woman, and with the experience of Brussels behind her, Ionanthe intended to equip herself with all the information she would need to enable her to work behind the scenes and improve the lot of the people.

Tonight's dinner, in honour of Philippe de la Croix, would be a good place for her to start honing the skills she would need.

The dinner was to be a formal event, and Ionanthe had dressed accordingly in one of the two designer evening gowns she had purchased for similar events in Brussels. The one she was wearing this evening was a deceptively simple column of dull cream heavy silk jersey that skimmed rather than hugged her body, with long sleeves and a high neckline slashed across her collarbone.

Luckily the ladies' maid the Count had found for her was a skilful hairdresser, and she had drawn Ionanthe's dark hair back off her face and styled it in a way that reminded Ionanthe of the Shakespearean heroine in a film she had once seen.

Her maid had insisted that the dinner necessitated the wearing of what she had described 'proper jewellery, from the Crown Jewels'.

Ionanthe had flatly refused to wear the heavy and ornate crown, opting instead for a far simpler tiara set, along with a diamond necklace and a pair of matching wide diamond cuff bracelets worn over the sleeves of her gown.

Since the castle could be cold, and it was a long walk

from the Princess's robing room, where the Crown Jewels were stored, to the reception and dining rooms in the newer part of the building, Ionanthe had agreed that she would need some kind of warm covering. She had, though, refused the ermine-lined cloak the maid had wanted her to wear, and was instead wearing a far simpler cloak in rich dark ruby velvet.

Max, who had gone through much the same arguments with his valet as Ionanthe had with her maid, felt his heart unexpectedly contract when he saw Ionanthe coming towards him down the long gallery. That she would look every inch a princess he had expected—but that she would do so with such elegance, stamping what was obviously her own style on the position she now held, caught at his emotions before he could check his reaction to her. Her sister's interpretation of regal splendour had been a wardrobe full of tight-fitting rhinestone-covered designer clothes—more suitable, in Max's opinion, for a media-attention-hungry C-list celebrity.

After Eloise's death he had instructed that the clothes be packed up and sent to an appropriate charity shop.

Max suspected that the dress Ionanthe was wearing had been chosen because she believed that its flowing style did not draw attention to her body. But as a man Max knew that the cream fabric's gentle skimming of her body drew the gaze far more intently than her sister's tight, cleavage-revealing clothes had ever done.

Had things been different—had they met in different circumstances, had they chosen freely to be together, had he been able to trust her in a way that would have made them true partners, working together for a shared cause—Max knew that this moment would have been very special indeed. In the privacy of their marital bed they would, for instance, already have discussed the French diplomat's visit, and would have agreed a shared plan for maximising its potential for the benefit of the people. Max was keen to explore the possibility of making more of the island's small wine-producing area, and Monsieur de la Croix belonged to a renowned dynasty of French wine-producers.

Ionanthe had almost reached him. Automatically Max went towards her, formally offering her his crooked arm.

Unable to stop herself, Ionanthe hesitated, and then mentally rebuked herself. What was there to fear, after all? She would not be touching his bare flesh, would she? She was wearing clothes, and Max, as hereditary holder of the office of Commander of the Royal Guard, was wearing its winter dress uniform—dark green jacket ornamented with gold frogged fastenings and gold epaulettes—whilst his second in command stood to one side of him holding the large plumed helmet that denoted Max's status.

The colour of dark green for the uniform had originally been chosen so that the men who wore it would merge with the pine trees of the island's mountains, where fighting had frequently taken place when rebels had had to be subdued.

Privately Ionanthe had always disliked the wearing of what was, after all, a symbol of what had been the oppression of the poorest people of the island by its richest. However, she was forced to admit that Max carried the uniform off unexpectedly well. He gave off an air free from the louche arrogance of his late cousin. Max was a man who did not need a fancy uniform to garner respect from others.

Her mouth felt uncomfortably dry with tension as she rested her fingertips as lightly as she could on his sleeve.

Together they traversed the long gallery—together, and yet so very far apart, Ionanthe acknowledged painfully as they made their journey in silence.

Only when they had reached the double doors that led to the Audience Chamber where the reception was to take place did Max give any indication that he was aware of her. He turned his head to look at her for a second as the liveried flunkeys pulled open the doors and the heralds in their gaudy medieval tabards blew a shrill clarion call to attention for the waiting audience. His free hand covered her gloved fingers. She had been wrong to think that the formal barriers of gloves and sleeves would protect her from being affected by his touch. If anything those barriers made things worse, because they caused her to compare the satisfaction of the sensation of naked flesh on naked flesh with the ache of frustration that came now with the layers of cloth between them.

The dinner was almost over. The gold plate and the Sèvres china commissioned by the same Prince who had been responsible for the baroque decor of the rooms in this eighteenth-century addition to the original castle still gleamed in the light from the three ornate chandeliers illuminating the room. That same light also struck brilliant reflections from the facets of the diamonds worn by the female guests.

The main course had been served accompanied by wine from the diplomat's family vineyards, which Max had chosen especially, and the mood around the table had grown as mellow as it was possible to be under such circumstances.

Ionanthe was listening dutifully to their guest. She had seen him once before in Brussels—very briefly—at a large corporate event, and was well aware of his reputation as a womaniser. As she listened intently to him her heart contracted on a sharp stab of emotion—but not because of the attention he was paying her. On the contrary, she found his compliments as unappealing as the deliberately sexual looks he was giving her. No, it was the subject of his current self-satisfied monologue that was causing her muscles to tighten with angry anxiety.

'So is it true, then?' he pressed her, obviously seeking confirmation of what he had heard. 'This talk that your husband plans to allow other countries to bid for a licence to mine your coal reserves?'

Ionanthe couldn't answer him. She was too busy trying to conceal her angry dismay. Fortenegro's coal reserves lay beneath land owned by the Crown but grazed by the sheep of some of the poorest people on the island. They would be made even poorer—destitute, in fact—if, as the diplomat seemed to think, Max had agreed to allow foreign corporations to mine the coal.

It was impossible for her either to ignore or deny the intensity of the anger and the sense of betrayal she felt. Not because she herself was personally in any way disappointed by Max's callous disregard of his people's needs—of course not—her feelings were on behalf of those people, against Max's betrayal of them.

Cosmo might have been a selfish, self-satisfied egotist, who had thought only of his own pleasure, but at least *he* had had the virtue of being too lazy to think of adding to his own personal wealth by further pauperising his people. Max, who was shrewder and more business aware, could do far more damage to the island than Cosmo had if he literally mined its assets for his own personal benefit.

The diplomat was still awaiting her response. 'I'm afraid I'm not the person you should be asking,' she responded with ease. 'It is my husband who rules Fortenegro.'

'Ah, but even a man who is a ruler can be putty in the hands of a beautiful and intelligent woman who herself knows how the business world works. Should there be future opportunities here of international interest I am sure any astutely managed conglomerate would want to court your personal support.'

Was the Frenchman sounding her out as a possible aide in the future asset-stripping of the island? Ionanthe concealed her outraged revulsion, and her desire to inform Monsieur de la Croix that she wanted to protect her country from exploitation, not assist in it. After all, it was far better to allow him to think they might be future allies. That way she would have more chance of learning what deals were being discussed—although she had no idea how she might prevent them. It sickened her to remember how she had felt in Max's arms now that she knew what he was planning to do.

It had been the Count's idea that Monsieur de la

Croix should be seated next to Ionanthe rather than the Prince himself, even though he was the guest of honour, and now, watching the other man focusing so intently on Ionanthe and quite obviously flirting with her, totally ignoring the elderly dowager on his left-hand side, Max was finding it more and more difficult not to watch them—like some passionately in love fool who was being ridiculously and unnecessarily jealous.

It was a relief to Ionanthe when the evening finally came to an end and the French diplomat was escorted to a car waiting to take him to the airport for his homeward flight. Tomorrow morning Max would be leaving for Barcelona from that same airport, and then in the afternoon she herself would be leaving for her ancestral home—the Castle in the Clouds as it was known locally, because of the height of the mountain range on which it was built.

Of course it wasn't really loneliness and disappointment she felt, she reassured herself later, as she lay alone in the bed she had so briefly shared with Max. How could she live with herself, after all, if she were to admit to those feelings for a man who stood for and championed so much that she hated and despised?

If she had any longings, then they were simply longings to conceive the son who now more than ever she knew she must have to protect the people. It was not the thought of Max himself that made her body quicken and her pulse race, whilst her flesh was seized with a thrill of aching need. It was her growing sense of urgency with regard to conceiving a son. The ache now flaring hotly inside her came from her impatience to conceive—

from the knowledge that she had to have the most intimate sexual contact there was with Max to achieve her ambition. Not from any desire for Max himself…

CHAPTER EIGHT

THEY had almost reached the airport. Max put down the geological survey reports which had only arrived that morning and leaned back in the seat of the large Mercedes. He had commissioned the reports some months earlier, when he had first come to the throne, having heard rumours that certain factions within his court had been making enquiries about the possibility of Fortenegro's mountainous region possessing reserves not just of coal but of other valuable minerals and ores as well. One of the most likely areas to yield the more valuable commodities, according to the reports, was the mountain land owned by the late Baron—now owned by his granddaughter, Ionanthe.

Max exhaled. He did not welcome having to be so suspicious. He placed a very high value on mutual trust, and it was an important principle of his foundation. However, he also valued instinct, and his instinct was telling him—as it had done right from the start—that Ionanthe had had an undeclared purpose in agreeing to marry him.

That undeclared reason could, of course, be something personal that would not impact on anyone other than herself. It might well be that he was being overly cautious. It might be that he'd simply have to put his thoughts to her for her to supply him with an answer to his question. Ionanthe might not even be aware of the value of what lay beneath the surface of her family's land.

On the other hand, it might also be that Ionanthe *did* know—she had worked in Brussels, after all, and would be well aware of the importance and the value of certain raw materials. It was possible that she was now playing for very high stakes with the island's natural resources, in a 'winner takes all' throw of the dice. Was she contemplating selling out those who depended on her? Or was he allowing the grit of an instinct that had jarred on him to grow into something that owed more to his imagination than true fact?

Legally, of course, she had every right to dispose of any riches on or in the land which she owned—although Max deplored the immorality of anyone depriving such a very poor people of their living to add to their own already extensive wealth. It was impossible for her to know of his very private wish to bring an end to such feudal ownership of huge tracts of the island by a handful of powerful families—and that included much of the land owned by the Crown—in order to give it instead to the people. He had already known and accepted that he would have to move very carefully and tactfully, unfortunately perhaps even in secret in the early stages of this endeavour. It was essential for its success that none of the resources were sold on to someone outside the island before he could complete the process.

Now the situation with regard to Ionanthe further

complicated the issue—and all the more so because Max knew that what had happened between them meant that he could not really trust his own judgement. It would forever be clouded by the desire he felt for her. Had that desire damaged his ability to judge her correctly? Already he had told himself that she was a giver, not a taker; already he was not just prepared but actively wanting to believe the best of her. But Max knew that he could not afford to let his emotions control his judgement. There was far too much at risk for that. Little though he liked doing so, he owed it to his people to look suspiciously upon Ionanthe's possible motives.

Was it possible that Ionanthe had married him to provide herself with a smokescreen behind which she could sell off the mineral rights she now owned? Was that why she wished to visit her family home? Had she deceived him all along with her apparent inability to control her sensuality, using it as a means to lull him into a false state of security?

No wonder history recorded so many long-dead monarchs as suspicious paranoids, Max thought wryly.

Ionanthe had been asleep when he had gone into the bedroom this morning, tempted by an emotion that should have had no place in his thinking to reveal his concern to her. Thinking about her now, it was that image that filled his head: her hair a dark silky cloud on the white pillow, her face free of make-up. She'd slept on, oblivious to his presence, whilst his body had been all too acutely aware of hers.

The need he was fighting was far more skilled at getting past his barriers than he was at maintaining them, Max recognized, as his body began its familiar assault on his mind. And it wasn't just his body that was susceptible, over-printed with its memories of her. His emotions were now at war within themselves as well. But when you stripped back everything else, it was trust, or rather the lack of it, that lay at the core of his dilemma. And not just his personal trust in her as a woman he was perilously close to loving. He was by virtue of his position the designated protector of his people's trust. Trust in himself and in those with whom he chose to share his most intimate confidences and beliefs. He might judge that his need for Ionanthe outweighed his wish that he could trust her, but he could not make that choice with his people's trust. That was a risk he must not and would not take.

In another couple of hours Ionanthe would be leaving for the mountains. Was it, as he had initially assumed, because she wanted to put some distance between them? Or did she have another, far more devious purpose?

He wasn't going to find the answer to his question in Barcelona.

He reached for his mobile phone, and then leaned forward to attract the attention of his driver.

CHAPTER NINE

SHE could have driven herself to the castle—she had wanted to. But the Count had protested that it was unseemly for her to do so in her new role, so Ionanthe had given in, even whilst reminding the Count that the road to the castle was badly maintained, and because of that it would be necessary for her to travel there in a sturdy four-wheel drive rather than the kind of car more suited for pomp and State occasions.

Initially she might have made the impetuous decision to visit her childhood home to escape from Max and her vulnerability to him, but Ionanthe hadn't forgotten the vow she'd made to herself to use the wealth she had inherited from her grandfather to improve the lives of their tenants and those who worked for the family. As an ambition it came nowhere near matching the truly awesome achievements of the Veritas Foundation she so admired, but it was a small step in the right direction. Ionanthe smiled ruefully to herself at the thought of the reaction of the chairman of Veritas in the unlikely event of him ever getting to know how much the foundation's achievements had inspired her.

It was a cornerstone of the foundation's ethos that inherited wealth should be used for the greater good of those people who were most in need—mainly through health incentives followed by education. The island had a desperately poor record on both issues. There was one exclusive private hospital for the rich, and a handful of shamefully ill-equipped and badly run clinics for the poor. The wealthy sent their sons abroad for private schooling and groomed their daughters for the right kind of marriage, whilst the poor—if they were lucky—made do with state education which ended when a child reached fourteen. Fortenegro did not have proper senior schools for its brighter children, never mind colleges or a university. There was no middle class. Any islander who did well enough to make any money tended to leave the island, seeking better opportunities for themselves and their families.

It could all have been so very different. Fortenegro was rich in natural assets, which included its mineral deposits, its climate, and its scenery.

Max would probably be in Barcelona by now. Ionanthe looked at the telephone on the desk. In a normal relationship a man separated from his partner would surely telephone her, ostensibly to assure her of his safe arrival, but in reality because of their shared need to hear one another's voice. But of course hers was not a normal relationship, and even less a normal marriage. Her own thoughts pressed on her heart like hard fingers on a painful bruise, making her want to withdraw from the hurt they were causing.

'Highness, the car is waiting.'

Ionanthe nodded her head in response to the Count's information.

The air was colder today—a warning that winter was almost here, Ionanthe recognised, as she looked up towards the hills already cloaked in snow.

In only a few days it would be Christmas. *Christmas.* She could feel the familiar sadness settling on her like the drift of winter snow. Christmas had once been her favourite time of year. But Christmas was a time for sharing, for loving, and she had no one with whom to share her love or the deepest secrets of her heart. She had no loving, caring family with whom to spend this special time of year.

In Brussels she had dreaded the build-up to the season, forced to listen and watch as her co-workers prepared excitedly for their Christmas break, talking of their happiness at the thought of 'going home' or being with someone special. Christmas could be the cruellest time of year for those without love, as she well knew.

According to the Count, the court made no special plans for Christmas; when Cosmo had been alive he had always spent from late December until the end of January away from Fortenegro, 'enjoying himself'.

Ionanthe burrowed deeper into the camel-coloured cashmere coat she was wearing—another item she had worked and saved hard for. Ionanthe was a believer in 'investment' items of clothing. Throw-away clothes, like throw-away relationships, held no appeal for her. Perhaps because of her childhood, she yearned for those things that would endure and on which she knew she could depend.

A little to her surprise, the waiting equerry was holding open the front passenger door of the sturdy four-wheel drive vehicle waiting in the courtyard. Its darkened windows were an affectation that made Ionanthe suspect that the vehicle must have been one of the many carelessly purchased by Cosmo.

Even more unexpected was the fact that the car was without its driver. But Ionanthe didn't realise that until she was in her seat and the equerry was closing the door and moving round to the driver's side of the vehicle, holding it open for the man now coming down the steps towards them.

Ionanthe's heart whooshed to the bottom of her ribcage as though caught up in an avalanche. Max! It surely couldn't be him? But it was! Just for a moment the sweetest and most intoxicating surge of joy filled her—but then reality cut in. He couldn't possibly have changed his mind because he wanted to be with her. And she shouldn't want that to be the case.

She watched guardedly as he got into the car, unable to stop herself from saying, almost accusingly, 'You're supposed to be in Barcelona.'

'I am supposed to be,' Max agreed. 'But my meeting was cancelled.' It was the truth, after all—even if he himself had been the one to do the cancelling. 'And I decided it would be a good idea if we were to visit your castle together. It will help to reassure people of our unity, and of course of our commitment to one another and to them.'

Ionanthe gave a small shiver, despite the delicious warmth of the car's interior. 'I really don't think that would be a good idea,' she protested.

'You don't? Why not?'

Why not? Because her escape had been about preventing any intimacy between them, not promoting it. But of course she could hardly tell him that.

'My grandfather didn't use the castle very much. It's old-fashioned, and not very well equipped with mod cons.'

'Really? I understood from your sister that your parents had spent what she described as "a fortune" on installing modern plumbing and central heating.'

Ionanthe's heart sank. Her parents *had* modernised the castle—much to the anger of her grandfather, who had never ceased complaining about what he considered to be a waste of money. Eloise had taken the same attitude as their grandfather, begrudging the money spent and claiming that such luxuries as bathrooms and central heating were wasted on the staff who looked after the castle.

'That was nearly twenty years ago. I'm not even sure the central heating system will still be working.'

'If it isn't then we shall just have to find some other way to keep warm, then, shan't we?'

The swift hiss of Ionanthe's betraying breath should have pleased him, but instead it made him feel like stopping the car and taking her in his arms.

To punish himself, Max continued briskly, 'After all, I'm sure your staff must have found one. It would be uncomfortable if not impossible for them to endure the cold of the mountain winters if they had not.'

Was Max genuinely expressing concern for others? Or was he simply using them as a means of mocking her?

'The boiler and the fires are fed by logs cut from trees that fall or have to be felled,' she explained. 'It is hard work, and the logs have to be eked out carefully when there are bad winters.'

'You make it sound very unpleasant, but I dare say those who live there are accustomed to it. Or do they wish for an easier life in a less harsh environment?'

Max's question made Ionanthe tense. What was the true purpose of his questions and his obvious determination to visit the mountains? Was he merely making conversation, or did he have a darker purpose in suggesting that her people might wish to abandon the mountains and live somewhere else? It was, after all, beneath the mountains that the coal lay—on land he owned, which bordered what was now hers.

What was he trying to prove in giving Ionanthe the opportunity to confide in him? Max wondered grimly.

She wasn't going to play Max's game, Ionanthe decided. She had already learned the painful cost of doing so, hadn't she?

'It is their choice to live where and how they do,' she answered, giving a small shrug as she did so in an attempt to express a lack of interest in the subject that would bring his questions to an end.

But Max gave her a hard look and suggested, in an even harder voice, 'And since *you* do not have to endure their hardship it is of no concern to you? Your sister expressed much the same view. I should perhaps have expected that you would share it.'

Was he trying to suggest that she didn't care about the lives of those who depended on her? Now Ionanthe was really angry.

'For your information, I do *not* slavishly adopt the views of others. I formulate my own. And if you knew anything about history then you would know that in many instances—from the Scottish Highland clearances to the wholesale movement of people from their terraced houses to the planners' rabbit hutch post-war flats—when people have been taken from their environment and resettled against their will it has led to the destruction of their sense of community, adding to their ills rather than lessening them. If my people wish to move and change their way of life then of course I shall do my best to aid them in that endeavour. But I will never force it upon them.'

There was real passion in her voice, Max acknowledged. Passion and conviction. But was there also honesty?

They were approaching the turn-off they needed to take from the coast road, but before Ionanthe could let Max know it was coming up he was signalling to make the turning.

As though he knew what she was thinking, he told her curtly, 'I visited the castle with Eloise, shortly before our marriage.'

'She wouldn't have liked that.'

The words were out before Ionanthe could stop them. Now he would think she was jealous and mean as well as everything else, Ionanthe thought miserably, unable to look at Max for fear of what she might see in his eyes.

'Eloise was always a city and bright lights person,' she explained lamely. 'Neither she nor our grandfather liked the castle.'

'But you did?' Max guessed.

'It was my family home when our parents were alive. My mother loved it, and because my father loved her he was happy for them to make their home there.'

Ionanthe's voice softened and warmed as she spoke of her parents. Eloise had barely spoken of them or her sister at all, Max remembered.

'My parents had so many plans—especially my mother. She wanted—' Abruptly Ionanthe stopped. That was what you got from allowing your emotions to take over. You were in danger of saying things it was best not to say. Her mother had been a reformist, a pioneer in her way, who had felt passionately about the importance of education and who had proved her commitment to her beliefs by setting up her own small school for the children of those who worked in the castle and on its lands. It had been Ionanthe's own special and much loved task to help the very little ones with their letters.

Watching the way her expression softened, Max thought she had never looked lovelier. Her emotions had brought a luminosity to her skin and her eyes, a sweet approachability that was not vulnerability but something stronger and deeper—as though a path had opened up between them. As though...

Lost in her memories, Ionanthe continued softly, 'At this time of year my mother would send my father out into the forest to bring back a Christmas tree. It had to be tall enough for the star to touch the ceiling in the grand hall, and its lower branches wide enough for there to be space beneath them for all the presents my mother would wrap for the children. She always seemed to know exactly what each child most longed for. Many of the toys were made in secret in the estate's carpentry shop—dolls' houses and cribs for the girls, forts and trains for the boys, puppets and so much more… We made our own decorations too—my mother was very artistic. The time around Christmas always seemed to be filled with our parents' laughter.

'At New Year my parents held a large party, with lots of guests coming to stay, but Christmas itself was always for the children. We'd have snow, of course, being in the mountains, and there'd be snowball fights and ski races. To me as a child Christmas was the best time—magical and filled with love and happiness. When my parents died it was as though they had taken Christmas with them, because it was never the same afterwards. That was when my grandfather moved permanently to his apartment in the royal castle.'

Her words had brought an ache to Max's throat, a need to open his arms to her and hold her safe within them, a longing to tell her that somehow he would find a way to make Christmases magical again. How on earth was he going to be able to stick to his principles if just listening to her talk about her childhood was going to put his judgement in the balance and weight the scales heavily in her favour?

Max told himself that he was glad that he was driving, because that at least stopped him from touching her. 'And you and Eloise? Where did you live after your parents' death?' he asked, trying to sound detached.

His question caused Ionanthe to look at him. Hadn't Eloise told him *anything* about their childhood?

'Grandfather took Eloise with him. They were always close.' She wasn't going to say that Eloise had been their grandfather's favourite and make herself sound even more pathetic and jealous. The plain, unwanted grandchild who had been pushed into the background to mourn the loss of the parents who had loved her as her grandfather had not.

'And you?' Max persisted. He was frowning now, as though angered by something.

'I went away to school. It was what I wanted and what my parents had always planned.'

No need to say that their parents had planned to send them both, not separate them and favour one above the other.

'What about you and your childhood?' Ionanthe asked him, wanting to divert their conversation away from herself.

'Me? I was an only child.'

'And your parents?'

'Dead. An accident.'

The curt voice in which the information was delivered warned Ionanthe not to pursue the subject—and yet she wanted to. Because she wanted to know all there was to know about him.

And so what if she did? Wasn't there an old adage about knowing one's enemy?

Enemies? Was *that* what they must be?

Whilst they had been talking the road had started to climb steeply. Small patches of snow lying in the hollows gradually became more widespread, until up ahead of them the whole landscape was white—apart from where the trunks of the trees were etched dark and the sheer face of the rocks showed grey with age.

A flight of geese cut their perfect V formation across the sky—heading, Ionanthe guessed, for the large natural lake that lay just below the snow line.

'Some of the older estate workers swear that there were once bears in the mountains,' she told Max with a small smile. 'But my father always used to say it was simply a story to scare us children.'

It had started to snow. Thick fat flakes drifting down from a grey sky. How she had once loved the first snows of winter, hoping they would fall thick and deep enough to keep her parents in the castle with them. She hadn't recognised then how hard the harsh weather made the lives of those who worked on the land—tenant farmers, in the main, with flocks of goats and sheep. If there was mineral wealth beneath these sometimes cruel mountains then surely it belonged to those farmers?

Christmas. He hadn't realised how close it was, Max admitted. The foundation had a special fund that provided money for various charities to help those in need at this special time of year.

Max remembered the year his parents had given him the best present he had ever received. He had been sixteen, and he could still remember the thrill of pride he had felt when they had told him that they were giving him his own small area of responsibility within the foundation. He had been given a fund-raising target to meet. He had delivered newspapers, cleaned cars and run errands in order to earn the money to make that target, and no target he had met since had been as sweet.

Because his parents had been killed shortly after his eighteenth birthday, and from then on there had been no one to praise him for his endeavours.

The four-wheel drive was equipped with snow tyres, and they were needed now that they were above the snow line.

They were nearly there. Once they had gone round the corner they would be able to see the castle. Ionanthe folded her hands in her lap. It was foolish to feel so excited. She wasn't a child any more, after all. Even so she caught and held her breath as they rounded the next bend, expelling it on a long sigh at the sight high above them, on its small plateau on the mountainside, of the castle, its topmost turrets disappearing into the heavy snow clouds.

It was truly a fairytale castle—all turrets and crenulated battlements, its exterior faced with a white limestone that made it look more as though it was made from icing sugar than the granite the facing concealed.

The small ornamental lake in the grounds where she had learned to skate would be frozen. Her parents had held skating parties there with coloured lanterns suspended from the branches of the trees that overhung the lake to illuminate the darkness. Ionanthe remembered lying in bed with her window wide open, despite the cold, so that she could listen to the adult laughter.

They had reached the long drive to the castle now, and the trees that bordered it were so heavy with snow that their branches swept right down to the ground.

The light had started to fade, and one by one the lights were coming on in the castle, to cast a warming welcoming glow from the windows. In the courtyard people were waiting for them, eager hands opening the car doors, familiar voices exclaiming proudly, 'Your Highness.'

Retainers she remembered as formidable adults not afraid to chide an over-active child were now bowing and curtsying low to her.

Impulsively Ionanthe reached out to take hold of the arms of the cook, remonstrating with her. 'No, Ariadne, please. There is no need.'

'Hah, I see you still hold the same republican views as your mother,' the elderly woman snapped sharply. 'Well, there are those of us who still respect our Sovereign, and if we want to show that respect then we shall.'

Max was hard put to it not to laugh. The small red-cheeked woman reminded him very much of a Greek cook his parents had once employed. She had run the whole household, and Max suspected that this woman did the same.

'So you're a republican at heart, are you?' He couldn't resist teasing Ionanthe as they were ushered inside.

'Ariadne likes to think so,' was all Ionanthe would allow herself to say.

The great hall was ablaze with lights, a fire roaring in the large fireplace, although Max suspected that it was the radiators that in reality kept the double-height room so warm.

The room's heat made Ionanthe frown and say accusingly to Ariadne, 'You've got the heating on.'

'Of course. You don't think we'd allow our Prince to freeze to death, do you?'

Ionanthe's lips compressed. She knew how much

wood it took to warm the great hall, and what back-breaking labour it was to provide that wood.

'I don't want you using a whole winter's supply of logs to keep the castle warm just because we're here,' she told Ariadne.

When they got back to the royal palace she must make arrangements, somehow, for extra supplies of wood to be delivered to the castle, to replace that which would be burned keeping the place warm for them, she decided.

'You needn't worry about that,' Ariadne assured her. 'Pieter has turned off all the radiators except those down here and in the drawing room—and in the state bedroom, of course. Made up the bed with that special linen your mother liked so much, Magda has.'

As the full meaning of Ariadne's words sank into Ionanthe's head, a trill of horror shot through her. 'You've put us both in the state bedroom?' she demanded.

'Well, of course I have. Where else would you sleep?' Ariadne demanded. 'Decorated especially for His Highness's great-grandfather, that room was.'

Ionanthe didn't dare look at Max.

'I suppose you'll be wanting Pieter and the men to go out and bring you a Christmas tree in? Wouldn't be a proper Christmas without one, after all. It's time we had you here for Christmas. A place isn't a proper home without family in it.'

Ionanthe listened to the older woman with growing dismay as she realised that Ariadne thought they were here for Christmas. Ariadne was attempting to sound disapproving, but Ionanthe could see how pleased she was. She hated having to disappoint her, but she would have to put her right and correct her misapprehension.

'Ariadne, this is only a brief visit—' she began. But to her astonishment Max put his hand on her arm and shook his head.

'What the Princess means, Ariadne, is that we are unable to stay as long as we'd like.'

'Well, as to that, it's the mountains that says how long a person stays. *You* should know that,' she reminded Ionanthe. 'You've been snowed in here often enough, after all. I remember the year that sister of yours kicked up such a fuss because she couldn't go to some party or other. Chasing after some boy, I expect, and in no mind to be stopped. Always spoiled, she was. The old Baron could never see her for what she really was. Always did favour shine over substance, he did. More fool him.'

Ionanthe shot a quick look at Max, wondering how he was reacting to Ariadne's criticism of Eloise, but it was impossible to guess his thoughts from his expression.

Ariadne hadn't finished. 'You'll find this one a different kettle of fish from the other,' she informed Max bluntly. 'You've got the better bargain with her.'

'I'm sure you're right,' Max agreed, keeping his face straight.

'I am right. Watched them both growing up, I did. That Eloise always did think too well of herself and not well enough of others. Of course this one's just the opposite—always putting others first. What you want, my girl, is a nursery full of little ones to keep you busy.'

Ariadne might be speaking to her, but she was looking

at Max, Ionanthe recognised, with a roguish glint in her
small currant-dark eyes. She'd even put her head on one
side, as though inviting Max to agree with her.

CHAPTER TEN

'BEFORE you complain, let me remind you that none of this is my fault. I didn't ask you to come here with me,' Ionanthe told Max sharply.

They were in the state bedroom, and the flush on Ionanthe's cheeks was caused more by her emotions than by the heat or the fire—even if she *was* desperately trying not to look as though she cared about the fact that the room possessed only one double bed, and not a particularly wide double bed at that.

'What exactly is it that you expect me to complain about?' Max asked quizzically.

Ionanthe gave him a suspicious look. 'You know perfectly well what I mean. We're going to have to share this…this room, or risk Ariadne making a dreadful fuss.'

Max grinned at her. 'Well, we certainly don't want that, do we? She might send us to bed supperless.'

To her own disbelief Ionanthe discovered that she desperately wanted to giggle.

'She can't help it,' she defended the elderly woman. 'She's always been the same. Grandfather used to get infuriated with her and threaten to sack her, but she'd just ignore him.'

'Sensible woman.' Max flicked back the heavy silk linen window hanging and informed her, 'It's still snowing.'

'Then you'd better work some royal magic to make it stop,' Ionanthe told him shortly, adding, 'I don't know why Ariadne assumed we'd be here for Christmas. I certainly never said that. When I telephoned I simply said that I'd be staying for a couple of nights.'

'It won't be the end of the world if we do have to stay, will it? Or do you have some special reason for wanting to leave?'

Ionanthe frowned. 'No, of course not. I was thinking of you. It will be expected that you spend Christmas at the palace.'

Max crooked one eyebrow and asked wryly, 'Why?'

For a reason Ionanthe didn't want to dwell on, something about the way Max was looking at her made her feel stupidly flustered—hot and flustered, she acknowledged. Treacherously, the image of a fig, luscious and ripe and dusted in sugar, slipped tauntingly into view inside her head. Now she didn't only feel flustered, she felt flushed as well—hot and flustered and— She licked uncomfortably dry lips. Surely this wasn't what was going to happen to her every time she was alone in a bedroom with Max?

Ionanthe struggled to replace the teasing image inside her head with a blank screen, knowing that she still hadn't answered Max's question and that he was quite obviously expecting her to do so.

'I wouldn't have thought that state business comes to a halt just because it's Christmas,' she eventually replied, in a stuffy, righteous voice she hardly recognised as her own.

Max looked less than impressed by her argument, one dark eyebrow inclining even more steeply. 'I can conduct what state business I have to attend to just as easily here as there. One of the benefits of modern technology,' he informed her dryly, indicating the Blackberry he had just removed from his jacket pocket.

Ionanthe took a deep breath in an attempt to steady herself, and was then forced to exhale it faster than she'd wanted when she saw that Max had turned away from her to remove the jacket of his business suit. The fabric of his shirt stretched across the breadth of his shoulders as he did so. Beneath that shirt lay flesh so smooth and honed that just looking at it was an intensely sensual experience, never mind what happened when she actually touched it—and him.

What was the matter with her? Hadn't she sat through innumerable business meetings during which men had removed their suit jackets without reacting like this?

But they hadn't been Max.

Like the muffled sound of a warning bell rung so hard and deep that its echo shook the depths, Ionanthe felt a tremor of warning deep within her body.

No! It was inconceivable that this man should be the one to affect her like this. The adage that it was too late to lock the stable door after the horse had bolted had surely never been more appropriate.

Ionanthe knew that if Max were to turn to her now and take her in his arms she would not be able to resist him—or herself. But when he did turn back to her he merely said casually, 'Didn't Ariadne say something about having made you some of your favourite soup?'

'You're hungry?' Ionanthe guessed.

She couldn't look at him. She was too afraid that he might see her disappointment and guess its cause. It was so unfair that, having taken flight here to protect herself from him, all she had done was leave herself more vulnerable. They would be thrown far more into one another's company here than they would ever have been at court.

Max studied Ionanthe's downbent head. The fall of her hair revealed a glimpse of the elegant length of her neck, her skin as luminous as a pearl. Desire flamed through him, hot and urgent. He wanted to go to her and draw her back against him, tasting the soft warmth of her skin as he did so, waiting for her to turn in his arms and press herself into him, silently saying that she shared his need, offering him her lips, herself, her love…

Her *love*? Was that really what the hunger gnawing at him was? A need not just for the sexual pleasure he had already shared with her, but for something richer and deeper, something stronger, more primitive and eternal?

Was he hungry? Ionanthe had asked, and the true answer was *yes*, he was. Hungry for Ionanthe. Hungry for exactly what he had told himself he must not want because of the danger attached to it.

How had it happened? Max had no idea.

'Yes, I'm hungry,' he agreed.

His voice was flat and hard, and for some reason it left Ionanthe with an ache in her throat and smarting eyes.

* * *

The large, comfortable kitchen was busy. A young woman whom Ionanthe vaguely recognised was whisking about, whilst two young children were seated at the table crayoning.

'You'll remember Marta, Gorge's youngest,' Ariadne informed Ionanthe, and the pretty young woman gave Ionanthe a shy smile. 'Married to our Tomas, she is now, with two young ones of her own.'

Ionanthe returned the young woman's smile.

'I'm teaching my two their letters, Highness, just like you taught me mine. Ever so grateful to you and your mother we were, for telling our parents that we should have our schooling. I've told my Tomas that our girls are going to get their schooling no matter what.'

Ariadne, who was stirring a large pot on the stove, gave a derisory snort. 'Soft as butter, Tomas is—not like fathers were in my day. Them parents of yours have a lot to answer for, filling folks' heads with ideas above their station with all that talk of schooling and the like.'

'Take no notice of Mam,' Marta told Ionanthe cheerfully. 'Proud as punch of our two girls, she is, and always telling them that they've got to pay attention to their lessons. Teachers is what I'd like them to be. But they'd have to go to the mainland for that, and that costs money.'

Watching Marta's bright smile give way to uncertainty and anxiety, Ionanthe reached out towards her, telling her without thinking, 'Don't worry, Marta. The money will be there for them. I'm planning to set up a fund in my parents' name, out of the money my grandfather left. It will provide scholarships for children like yours to get all the education they need.'

It was Ariadne who spoke first in the silence that followed Ionanthe's impulsive declaration, saying triumphantly to her daughter-in-law, in whose eyes emotional tears were beginning to glisten, 'There—you see. I told you our Princess would see to it that something was done. Not that you'll have an easy time persuading *some* folk to send their children to school,' Ariadne added darkly.

'All the children of Fortenegro should have the right to a good education. It is my duty as Fortenegro's ruler to ensure that they do.'

Max's voice was firm and uncompromising, causing them all to look at him.

'My wife is to be applauded for what she plans to do, but there must come a day when the children on this island receive their education as a right, not as a gift.'

Ionanthe couldn't take her gaze from Max's face. They might almost have been alone as her expression showed him how much his declaration meant to her.

'Do you really mean that?'

'Yes,' he confirmed.

CHAPTER ELEVEN

'CONVINCING the barons and some of the community elders that no child should leave school before sixteen won't be easy, never mind winning them round to the idea of Fortenegro having its own colleges and university,' Ionanthe warned Max.

They were alone in the great hall, having just finished their dinner, and Ionanthe's face was flushed with delight and the hope that Max really shared her belief that changes needed to be made, allowing the children of the island to receive the educational opportunities they were currently denied.

'There will be opposition, I know,' Max allowed.

'A great deal of opposition,' Ionanthe agreed.

She paused. The French diplomat's comment about the licensing of coal mining was a spectre she desperately wanted to banish.

'What you're planning will be very expensive,' she began hesitantly. 'You will need to increase the island's revenue to the Crown.'

'I have several plans in mind for that,' Max told her. Should he bring up the subject of the mineral reserves on her land? He wanted to do so. The realisation that she shared at least one of his plans, and the sense of being at one with her that had created over dinner, made him want to be open and honest with her. But now was perhaps not the time for a further potentially lengthy discussion.

The fire was burning low; Ionanthe was smothering a small yawn. There were more intimate ways in which he wanted to communicate with her right now; more personal bonds he wanted to forge with her.

'You're tired?'

Max's words were a statement, not a question, and the smile which accompanied them made Ionanthe's heart leap and flounder inside her chest.

'Yes,' she admitted.

'We've travelled a long way today, sometimes over difficult and unfamiliar territory, but for my own part I have to say that the journey has been very worthwhile,' Max told her, before emphasising softly, '*Very* worthwhile.'

Ionanthe looked at him and saw that she had been right to sense that he was not referring to their journey to the castle.

'I agree,' she responded, picking her words as carefully as she could.

From the smile Max was giving her, it had obviously been the response he wanted.

'Time for bed?' he suggested.

Ionanthe struggled to control the leap of delight in her body.

'I'm sorry that Ariadne has put us both in the same room.'

Max stood up and came towards her, reaching down to take her hand and pull her gently out of her chair.

'Are you? That's disappointing. Perhaps I can persuade you to change your mind?'

Ionanthe's breath caught in her throat, her thoughts a giddy whirl of mingled disbelief and excitement. Did Max really mean what he seemed to be saying? The evening and their shared conversation had brought them so close that for her there was only one way she wanted it to end.

It was because it was so cold on the stone stairs and walking down the long passage that led to their room in the tallest turret tower of the castle that they had to walk so close together, with Max's arm around her, holding her close to his side. That was what Ionanthe told herself, but it was not a valid excuse for what happened outside their bedroom door, when Max pulled her into his arms and kissed her.

'You taste of cold mountain air and magic,' Max told her, tracing the shape of her lips with the pad of his thumb.

'Magic hasn't got a taste,' Ionanthe objected huskily.

'Yes, it has,' Max corrected her. 'It tastes of wonder and witchery and woman—the woman I want more than any other woman I have ever wanted before.'

Ionanthe couldn't believe what she was hearing. She hardly dared breathe in case she broke what she knew must be some kind of spell.

Her eyes dark with emotion, she asked, 'Do you want me more than you wanted Eloise?'

There was a small pause, during which she trembled

and Max's arms tightened around her, and then he answered her truthfully.

'There is no comparison.'

He kissed her again, his mouth hot and hard on hers, before he withdrew from her to say gruffly, 'I can't kiss you as I want to out here, and if I don't stop now I won't be able to.'

They were inside the room and Max was locking the door. The room's warmth welcomed them, the soft glow of the fire casting softly caressing shadows.

Ionanthe went to the window and drew back the heavy curtain to perch on the small window seat and look out. Almost immediately Max joined her, coming to stand behind her, his body close to hers and his hand on her shoulder.

'It's still snowing,' Ionanthe announced.

'Yes,' Max agreed, turning her to him.

There were no figs this time, but Max said softly that he didn't care, that Ionanthe herself was all he needed and wanted.

Ionanthe couldn't bring herself to voice her own feelings. She was half afraid that doing so might break the spell that was binding them together. It was enough that he was there and they were together.

The dying embers of the fire in the grate threw out enough light for her to see as well as feel the muscles and the strength of Max's body as she caressed him with secretly avid hunger and delight. Now she could marvel at the ease with which he could arouse her to those heights she had never imagined existed, instead of fearing it as she had done that first time.

They touched and caressed and kissed in a sensual warmth of absorbed pleasure, accompanied by the music of their soft sounds of mutual arousal which grew less soft and more urgent as their passion took fire.

The touch of Max's hand cupping the underside of her breast whilst his thumb-tip rubbed slowly against her nipple had Ionanthe crying out to him in sweet pleasure. When his lips took possession of her eager flesh in response to that cry Ionanthe held his head to her breast, arching her back in delight. Their bodies threw erotic shadows on the wall.

This time Ionanthe was bolder, determined to take her own pleasure from caressing and tasting Max as ardently as he had done her. Experimentally she drew her fingertips along the inside of his thigh—just the merest brushing of her nails in slow circles that at first held him rigid and then, when she persisted, drove him to groan and offer himself up to her with an intimate longing she couldn't resist.

Her lips followed her fingertips, until Max groaned out loud and pulled her to him.

She was eager and ready for him, welcoming the feel of him sinking deep into her, holding him there so that she could savour the sensation.

In silence they held one another, neither of them moving.

This was where he was meant to be—here, with this woman who made him feel that holding her like this was worth more than a thousand kingdoms, Max admitted to himself. It was too late now for him to tell himself that he mustn't love her. He *did* love her. He loved everything about her.

Now. Now she was whole and complete—holding Max to her and within her, Ionanthe acknowledged. She loved him more than she had thought it possible to love anyone.

They breathed together and their flesh quickened. Max began to move, driven by an age-old need, and Ionanthe opened herself to him, obeying a primitive instinct of her own.

Their pleasure rose and then plateaued, allowing them to rest their sweat-soaked bodies and ease their laboured breathing. The climb had been steep and urgent, claiming from them everything they had to give. And then, as though nature herself had grown impatient with the delay, the very act of their breathing set off within Ionanthe a small but cataclysmic tightening of eager muscles accompanied by a ripple of pleasure. Her hands tightened on Max's shoulders and immediately he responded, driving hard, feeling her taking him deep within her. Their rhythm changed, tightening, hurrying, rushing frantically as they laboured to meet the demands being made on them.

The end came fiercely, with a final paroxysm of shared pleasure leaving them clinging together at the pinnacle, their hearts thudding in unison.

Ionanthe woke to a morning of snow-bright light and the gentle caress of Max's hands on her body.

How delicious it was to wake to such sensual pleasure. She turned to Max and smiled sleepily at him, her smile turning to a soft gasp when his touch grew more intimate.

'We'll be late for breakfast,' she warned him.

'Mmm…breakfast, or this and you?' Max murmured, as though pretending to consider his choice.

His lips feathered kisses against her skin and his fingers teased nipples that were already showing how eager they were for him to make *them* his choice.

CHAPTER TWELVE

'I THOUGHT that since we shall have to spend Christmas here now, after last night's snowfall, we could perhaps have a party for everyone here at the castle on Christmas Eve. My parents used to do it.'

'It sounds a good idea to me,' Max agreed.

'We'll need a Christmas tree, of course.'

'I'll take some of the men and see what we can find.'

They exchanged smiles.

They'd breakfasted on homemade bread and honey from the estate's bees, whilst Ionanthe explained to Max that the estate was almost self-sufficient.

'The people live simply, but well, in the same way they have lived for many, many generations. That is why the elders of the communities are so opposed to change. They cannot see what benefits it could bring. They believe they have everything they need. They cannot see that we live in different times, and that they are denying the younger generation the right to make their own choices. They think that life can continue as it has always done without any change for ever, but it can't. The world is growing smaller; the island itself will have to change. That is inevitable.'

Max put down his coffee cup. Was one of the changes Ionanthe was envisaging the mining of the island's minerals? Last night, hearing her speak so passionately about the need for education for the island's children, he had admired and applauded her, allowing his heart to rule his head, but now once again the responsibilities of his role were reminding him that there were questions that had to be answered.

'When you say that the island will have to change, what kind of changes do you have in mind?' he asked.

Ionanthe shook her head.

'There are so many. Fortenegro has many natural resources—'

'And you favour utilising them?'

'I think that we have to. But in a controlled way, of course.'

'Of course.' Max's heart had grown colder with every word Ionanthe uttered. 'Have you thought of the disruption this will cause to people's lives? The antagonism there will be?'

'Yes, but it is still my belief that it must be done.'

Something was wrong. Ionanthe could sense it. The warmth had gone from Max's voice, and although he hadn't actually said anything critical Ionanthe felt that inwardly he was hostile.

Why, when last night they had seemed so much in accord? Was it that despite his apparent enthusiasm yesterday he was now having cold feet?

It hurt to think that the closeness she had believed they shared could vanish so easily.

She wasn't going to change her mind or backtrack, though. She couldn't—no matter how much she loved him. She owed it to the children of Fortenegro to stick to her plan. Marta's comments last night had shown her that.

She lifted her chin and told Max firmly, 'And here on this estate—my estate and my land—I intend that it *shall* be done.'

'No one can dispute that you have that right.' Max's voice was clipped and sharp. He wanted to get her to reconsider, to tell her that he would give her all the money she could want if only— If only what? If only she would be the woman he wanted her to be?

Max had enough experience of the world to know that there were far more people who would do exactly as Ionanthe planned to do, were they in her shoes, than those who would not. He couldn't blame her. Not really. If he wanted to blame someone then he should blame himself, for wanting her to be different, for wanting her to be the woman he had created out of his own need for her to be that way. And he didn't want to admit that it was possible for him to love a woman who did not share his outlook on life or his fierce attachment to working for the benefit of others.

Ionanthe hadn't deceived him. He had deceived himself.

Sitting alone in the castle library, Ionanthe closed her eyes to control the sting of unwanted tears. She hadn't wanted to come back to Fortenegro, after all, or to fall in love with Max. But now that she was here she had a duty to her people. They were the ones who really deserved the fortune her grandfather had left to her. Blood money, in her view, tainted with the blood, sweat and tears of those who had worked all their lives to earn it for her family without getting anything in return.

Last night, discussing her plans with Max, she had felt buoyed up with hope and the joy of sharing her dreams with him. She had felt as though everything she longed to do was possible and achievable, because she had thought he felt the same. But now, this morning, with that joy stripped from her, she felt as though she had a mammoth task in front of her and she wondered if she would ever achieve it.

If the reality was that Max was opposed to reform, then what chance had she of seeing it happen even here on her own land? The old guard—the barons and the community elders—would oppose her every step of the way.

Had she forgotten that it was because of that that she had agreed to marry Max? She had known then that an island like Fortenegro, locked fast in ancient tradition and a paternalistic society, could only be reformed by a very strong man. Her son. The son who would have to be what his father was not.

Then she had not cared about what Max was not, but neither had she known that she would love him, and that it would hurt her more than anything else ever had or ever would to know that there was this divide between them.

Max had gone out with the men to seek out a suitable Christmas tree. Ionanthe had watched him in the courtyard from the shelter of the kitchen, as he trod through the snow wearing an old pair of her father's ski boots.

Some of the men who worked on the estate, summoned by Tomas, Marta's son, had quickly gathered around him, making awkward semi-bows and tugging on dark tufts of hair exposed to the sharp wind as they removed their caps. They had responded to him, respecting him, respecting his natural air of authority, willing to let him take charge in a way they would never have done with her.

Wasn't there a saying that the hand that rocked the cradle ruled the world? Women like Marta were the future; they and their children had to be.

How much did it cost to build a school? To provide it with teachers and equipment? To provide its pupils with further education, with university education? The Veritas Foundation was helping to build and finance educational projects every day of the week. Ionanthe longed for just a fraction of their expertise, and for the dedication and the wisdom of the mystery man who was responsible for it.

She could understand why he clung to his anonymity, but nevertheless she wished that she might meet him. To speak with such a man must be a little like sitting at the feet of a very wise guru.

Ionanthe got up from her seat and looked out of the window. It had started to snow again. The library overlooked the castle gardens, and the snow there was pristine and untouched.

Already she was missing Max. She left the library and, although she could have sworn it wasn't what she had intended, for some reason she headed for the bedroom, frowning when she saw that the window was open. Snow had blown in and was covering the laptop case Max had left on the window seat.

Automatically Ionanthe picked it up, brushing the snow off with her hand as she did so. At the same time she accidentally dislodged some papers which must have been in the case's outer pocket. As she made to push them back, Ionanthe glanced at them and then stiffened.

Very carefully she sat down and pulled the papers free of the case, her hands trembling as she read the report she was holding—a report on the mineral assets of Fortenegro.

The sick feeling within her intensified, making her shake with a mixture of mouth-drying nausea and a longing to run away like a child and hide from what she did not want to see.

But she was not a child. And no matter how hard her heart might pound, or how much despair she might feel, she had to read on.

Frantically Ionanthe flicked through it, searching for what she hoped she would not find even whilst somehow knowing that she would. After all, hadn't this been what she had dreaded ever since Philippe de la Croix had told her about the coal mining consortium's approach?

And finally there it was—a full-page map of the mountains, *her* mountains, showing quite clearly where the rich veins of mineral deposits lay beneath them. The salient facts were there in print, heavily underlined as though to remind the reader of their importance.

Was this why Max had married them both? First her

sister and then her? Because he had *known* the value of
what lay beneath the harsh granite? Did he, like so many
others, value that more than he valued the rights of the
people who lived on that land? More than he valued her
and what they might have had together?

She couldn't cry. She had gone beyond that. But
inwardly she was weeping hot tears that blistered her
heart and would leave it forever scarred.

She had been a fool, of course; she had known from
the start—from that first sharply dangerous and sweetly
alluring spark of reaction to him which she had felt at
their first meeting and then denied—that her feelings
would lead to this pain. Hadn't she tried to guard against
her own vulnerability by giving herself a higher purpose
in agreeing to marry Max than merely her own safety
and that treacherous spark? Shouldn't she have stuck to
the path she had chosen then, and ignored the fatal
temptation to stray from it? If she had, then what she
had just read would only have strengthened her resolve
to help her son to be a very different man from his
father. If she had, then right now she would be feeling
justified and vindicated in her choice of action, not
guilt-ridden and heartbroken. She had no one but herself
to blame.

Oh, but she hurt so badly—quite literally sickened by
the incontrovertible evidence that Max was not worthy
of the love and trust of either her or, more importantly
by far, his people.

Given free choice she would have fled then, as fast
and as far as she could, seeking somewhere to hide
herself away from her pain. But she could not do that.

She must stay and face what had to be faced for the sake of those who could not protect themselves. She must stay and stand between Max and his plans. She was the only person who could, since the land belonged to her. She must not allow him to seduce her into giving away her people's rights in the same way that he had seduced her into giving him her love.

The door opened and Max came in.

'I think we've found you your tree, but you'd better come and inspect it before we bring it in,' he began, only to stop when he saw the report Ionanthe was holding.

'You've been through my papers?' he accused her.

'No.' Ionanthe denied his accusation fiercely, shaking her head. 'Someone left the window open and there was snow on your laptop case. I merely intended to move it out of harm's way. The papers fell out.' When she saw the cynical look he was giving her she cried out, 'It's the truth. Not that I have any need to justify myself to you now that I've seen what you plan to do.'

'What *I* plan to do?'

'You can't deny it. I've seen the evidence with my own eyes. When Philippe de la Croix told me he'd heard rumours that you were going to foreign conglomerates about a coal mining contract I wanted to believe that he was wrong, that unlike Cosmo you *don't* see the island simply as a means of filling your own bank account. No wonder you were so keen to marry both of us. You *knew* about the mineral ore and you wanted to make sure that you had a legal right to it. That's why you took me to bed and seduced me, making me believe that there could

be something more between us than merely a cold
dynastic marriage. And I dare say that's why you went
out with the men this morning as well. What were you
really doing? Trying to take rock samples? Well, you
were wasting your time. I would only ever allow this
land to be mined if it was the wish of those who live on
it, for *their* benefit, to provide them and their children
with all those things that the rule of your family has
denied them. No, don't come near me,' she told him
when Max closed the door and started to walk towards
her. 'I don't want you anywhere near me.'

'Have you finished?' Max's voice was even, but there
was a white line of anger round his mouth.

'Finished? I've finished thinking that I can trust you
to do the best for the people of Fortenegro, and I've certainly finished feeling that I can respect you, if that's
what you mean.'

'For your information I did not commission that
report, as you have accused me, because I want to benefit
personally from the island's resources. Far from it.'

'I don't believe you,' Ionanthe told him flatly.

'That is your choice. But think about this. I too heard
about plans to sell off the island's mineral assets to
benefit the few who owned them.'

'So you thought you'd get in on the act?' Ionanthe
interrupted him contemptuously.

'No such thing. In fact the very accusations you are
laying against me are exactly those that I should lay
against you. *You* are the one who will stand to benefit
if the minerals lying beneath your land are to be mined.'

Ionanthe was too shocked to conceal what she felt,

and her response betrayed her emotions. 'You thought that of me?'

'Why not? Both your grandfather and your sister proved themselves to be duplicitous, intent on putting their own interests first. Why should you be any different?'

Max knew that he was goading her, but he had to be sure she was saying what he thought she was saying.

'But I am not like them. You said yourself that you knew that I was different.'

Ionanthe's reaction was everything he'd hoped for. Even if she had originally thought about selling her mineral rights she would change her mind, see things differently, come to understand and share his views, share all those things he wanted to do for the island and those who lived there. She *must* care about them. She had already shown that in the way she had spoken about the need for more schools. But he must be sure. He must hear her say categorically that she had no ulterior motive for marrying him.

'You could have been deliberately deceiving me— deliberately creating a fake persona for yourself to conceal your real intentions. When there are millions at stake, then people…'

'You really think I would take that money for myself when the people need it so much, to pay for education and health care and a better infrastructure?' Tears burned her eyes.

'You had no real reason to come back to Fortenegro,' Max pointed out. 'You must have known that by doing so the feudal law of atonement would be invoked against you.'

'I knew it existed, yes, but it never occurred to me that a modern man of the twenty-first century would be governed by it. Were you the ruler you should be, you would have such antiquated laws repealed.'

Her unexpected attack on him hit a raw nerve. He would already have repealed those laws had he felt that the people would accept such changes. He still intended to repeal them—once he had won their trust.

'Such an act would merely have been empty words,' he felt obliged to tell her. 'It takes the will of the people to make a law work, and as you must know there any many people here on Fortenegro who, either through fear or ignorance or pride, or a mixture of all those things, are not willing to relinquish the control and power they believe such demanding laws give them. Do not deny it. That mindset is operating here within this castle and its lands every time a father refuses to allow his child an education. You have as good as said so yourself.'

'They do that because they have no choice.' Ionanthe immediately defended her people. 'Because they cannot afford to take their children off the land. Because the law allows landowners to demand a set number of days of work per year from their tenants.'

When Max didn't respond she shook her head in angry despair.

'Oh, it is hopeless trying to make you understand.' Tears of frustration gathered in her eyes. 'The other night when we were discussing education you let me think that you shared my views and my hopes for the people,' she accused him. 'But you were just deceiving me. Why would you do that if not to lull me into a false sense of security? To make me think that we shared a similar purpose?'

'I could just as easily use that argument against *you*,' Max told her curtly.

He shouldn't be doing this, Max knew. As Fortenegro's ruler, he knew he had a duty of care to his people which involved questioning her motives and acting on his suspicions. But he wasn't just Fortenegro's ruler. He was also a man. And as that man who had held her in his arms, who had known whilst holding her there that he never wanted to let her go, surely he had a duty to that feeling?

There was only one thing he could do now—one question he had to ask. The whole of his future personal happiness was balanced on the answer.

Ionanthe possessed strength of will, she possessed courage, and she was passionate about what she believed in. He could think of no one better to share both his personal and his public life. But he also had to know that he could trust her with Fortenegro's future; he had to know that she would put what was best for the island above her own personal gain. He could not and would not blame her for wanting to realise the wealth beneath the surface of her land for herself. From what he had learned, it was her grandfather who was to blame. He had taught his granddaughters to value wealth and pride, and to follow his example of always putting himself first.

'If you are not lying about the mineral deposits, then tell me that you had no ulterior motive whatsoever in agreeing to marry me other than the need to protect your own safety.'

Ionanthe looked at him, her expression anguished. She desperately wanted to win his trust, but lying was an anathema to her. She hesitated, and then admitted, 'I did have an ulterior motive, yes. But—'

Max didn't want to hear any more. He had been a fool to hope that he might be wrong. He turned back towards the door, but Ionanthe moved faster.

'You will listen to me,' she told him. 'Because for the sake of my people I cannot allow you to think what you are thinking. I did have an ulterior motive, yes, but it was *not* the one of which you are trying to accuse me. This island has a long history of rulers who have abused their position, and its people have suffered as a result. As you have said yourself, they are set in their ways and bound by ancient customs and laws which imprison them in a feudal system that denies their children so very much. I grew up witnessing that. I saw my parents' attempts to change things, and I saw the power of those who opposed those changes—including my own grandfather. I saw greed and pride and a lack of compassion. And I saw too that what this island needed more than anything else was a ruler strong enough and courageous enough to lead his people to freedom.

'When I heard that Fortenegro had a new ruler in you, I hoped so much that you would be that man—but then you married my sister, a woman I knew to be rapacious and selfish. Had you married her because you shared her belief that the island existed merely to fund her expensive lifestyle? I wondered. Or did you love her without sharing her views? I knew she did not love you. She wrote to me and said so. But then Eloise loved only herself, and the blame for that lay with our grandfather. I watched to see what changes you might make to benefit the people of Fortenegro, but I could find none. So I compared you with the man I admire more than any other man who walks this earth and I found you wanting.'

Max was shocked by the violent surge of savage male jealousy that gripped him to hear Ionanthe speaking of admiring another man.

In a manner that was completely out of character for him, he demanded contemptuously, 'And who *is* this paragon you so admire? Some Brussels eurocrat who makes laws he himself will never have to obey and plays God with other people's lives?'

Ionanthe's breath hissed out in furious denial.

'No. He is not. He is a man who works selflessly for the benefit of others. Through the auspices of the foundation which he heads he has heard and answered the cries of the poor and the sick. He has viewed them with compassion and understood their need. He has provided money for wells for clean water, for schools to educate, for hospitals to heal, for crops to grow and for peace, so that all those who use what he has given them can flourish.'

The passion in her voice showed how she felt, and Max had to look away from her. What she had just told him changed everything—but he could not tell her that.

Ionanthe's throat hurt, and her eyes ached with the tears she was not going to let Max see.

'Once it was my dream and my hope that I might work for the Veritas Foundation and learn from such a master. That was not to be, but there is *something* I can do for the people of Fortenegro, even if it is merely a small shadow of what he has done. Just as he educates the children of today so that they can grow to be to the leaders of tomorrow, I thought that as your wife *I* could provide Fortenegro with the ruler it so desperately needs.'

'You planned to convert me to follow the teaching of this…this man you admire so much?' he suggested.

Ionanthe shook her head.

'No. I hoped to conceive and raise a son who would be all the things that he will need to be to help this island. *That* was my hidden agenda in marrying you. No scheming to sell off the minerals that lie beneath the mountains,' Ionanthe told him on a slightly shaky breath.

She had wanted those last words to sound proud and scornful, but she was miserably aware that in reality they sounded closer to tearful and upset.

Battling through the complex mass of emotions Ionanthe's speech had aroused in him, for the first time in his life Max simply did not know what to say or do to make things right. He knew what he wanted to say; he knew what he wanted to do. But he also knew that the very last thing Ionanthe would want to hear from him right now was that her hero—the man she admired more than any other, the man she had placed on a pedestal and at whose feet she had openly and proudly confessed she yearned to sit and learn—was no other than himself.

Giving her that news now would hurt her dreadfully. Fiercely Max blinked away the telltale moisture that would have betrayed how much the thought of her pain hurt him.

It wasn't that he had deliberately set out to deceive her. No, it was simply that it had never occurred to him that it might be necessary for him to tell her about the foundation and his role in it.

He breathed in, and then exhaled.

'So you agreed to marry me hoping that I would give you a child—a son who, with your guidance, would in time become the ruler you believe the island needs?'

He sounded remarkably accepting of her plan, Ionanthe acknowledged, but instead of reassuring her that only served to increase her hostility and pain.

'Yes,' she confirmed.

'And those times when you lay in my arms, when my body possessed yours, for you it was only because you wanted me to give you my child?'

Ionanthe's heart bumped treacherously into her ribs. She looked at Max, and then wished she hadn't.

'Yes…of course.' Something about the way in which Max was looking back at her drove her into adding recklessly, 'What other reason could there be?'

Max's silence made her nerve-endings prickle with tension.

Please God, don't let him tell her mercilessly and truthfully that he *knew* from the minute he had touched her she had had no thoughts in her head for anyone or anything but him and the need he aroused in her.

'And now—if I have? If you *are* carrying my child?'

The question slipped under her guard and made her eyes widen and her heart thud.

'It's…it's too soon to know,' she protested.

'That was not what I asked you,' Max pointed out. 'You have told me of your plans for my son's adult future, but what of his childhood? You have said nothing of that.'

Ionanthe frowned.

'What I want to know is how will he grow up?'

'What do you mean?'

'You and I both lost our parents before we were fully adult. You were pushed into the shadows by a grandfather who lavished all his attention on your sister. You must know as I do how much every child yearns for the security of being loved?'

'Yes, of course I do. I shall love my son.'

'But you do not love me, and he will sense that and be confused and hurt by it. Children always are when their loyalties are claimed by two parents who are opposed to one another.'

Both Max's voice and his expression were grave and heavy.

He genuinely cared about the emotional welfare of a child who might never exist, Ionanthe realised, with a small ache of surprise and sadness.

'You've been so long I've had to come and find you, and it's a long walk from my kitchen.'

Ariadne's arrival as she puffed towards them brought an immediate end to their conversation.

'The men are still waiting for you to come and look at the tree,' she told Ionanthe in a chivvying voice.

'I'll come and look now,' Ionanthe said.

'Christmas trees! A whole lot of fuss and bother, if you ask me,' Ariadne complained.

CHAPTER THIRTEEN

THE Christmas tree was a perfect fit, with the star which Max had placed on its topmost branch just touching the ceiling of the great hall. Its branches were now decorated with the homemade garlands and painted cones that she and the children had been busy making for the last two days, along with the familiar decorations Ionanthe remembered from her own childhood.

She touched one of the fragile glass baubles with a tender finger. It was from the set that her parents had bought one year when they had taken them to a German Christmas market. The bauble might be slightly tarnished, but Ionanthe saw it with the eyes of love and it was still beautiful. Just looking at it reminded her of the smell of warm gingerbread and the wonderful warmth of her father's large hand holding her own.

So many happy memories of a childhood in which she had felt loved and safe until her parents' deaths. Her mother and father had adored one another. Even as a young child she had somehow sensed that and been warmed by it. Ionanthe frowned. She was *not* going to allow Max's comments underlining the fact that he did not love her and that any child they had would suffer because of it to affect her.

They were still sharing the same bedroom and the same bed, but for the last two nights, since the confrontation between them in the library, they had slept in it as though they were miles apart. Max hadn't made one single move to approach her, or to apologise for what he had said. She certainly wasn't going to be the one to approach *him*. After all, she had done nothing wrong.

Except plan to bring up his son and heir to ultimately act against him and everything she thought he stood for.

It wasn't easy trying to pretend that nothing was wrong, but for the sake of the children so excitedly waiting for Christmas, and for the sake of their parents and grandparents who had made it plain how thrilled and honoured they felt to have them both here, Ionanthe felt that she had to make an effort. It was hard when she was having to strive desperately to pretend that she felt nothing for Max other than anger and contempt when the truth was—

Blindly she stepped backwards, gasping in shock as she bumped into the heavy wooden step ladders she had forgotten were there, striking her funny bone against one of the steps. A wave of nauseating dizziness from the sharply acute pain surged over her, causing her to sway slightly.

Max, who had been talking to Tomas, saw Ionanthe bump into the ladders and then clutch at her elbow, her face losing its colour as she swayed giddily. Immediately he hurried to her side, taking hold of her hand and demanding, 'Are you all right?'

'Of course I'm all right,' Ionanthe lied, trying to pull free.

The truth was that she felt terribly weak and sick, and would have given anything to rest her head on Max's shoulder and feel his arms close round her.

'All I did was catch my elbow,' she continued, when he refused to let her go.

A surge of love for her so strong that it felt as though it was drawn from the deepest core of him rolled over Max. Initially, in the aftermath of their quarrel, he had handled things badly, Max admitted to himself. He had spent most of the previous night lying awake, longing to turn back the clock. And not just because of the suspicions they'd had, the misjudgements they had both made about one another which had led to their quarrel.

Ionanthe's impassioned outburst about the Veritas Foundation and the man who controlled it, her obvious partisanship and admiration for both the organisation and the man behind it had, even if she herself could not know it, put him in a completely untenable position. He could not in all good conscience continue to withhold the truth from her—but how was he to tell her?

She was very angry with him, and her pride was hurt by his misjudgement of her. He knew that and he understood why. But that meant that this was not a good time to tell her that the man she so admired and had put on a pedestal, scornfully telling her husband of her hero's moral and charitable achievements, and how far short of him he fell, was actually the same man—him. She would be justifiably angry and—far more important to him—she would also be hurt.

On the other hand, if he didn't tell her, now that he knew how she felt, wasn't he going to be guilty of an even less excusable offence? One which in the long term would cause even more damage to their relationship because it would inflict a wound that would fester? They needed to be able to *trust* one another if the love Max was sure they felt for one another was going to be able to grow and flourish.

His only excuse for his omissions and failures was that he had never loved before, and that therefore everything he was learning was new. No matter how careful he was, no matter how much he wanted her happiness before anything else, he was fallible and liable to make mistakes.

Right now what they needed more than anything else was the two things they did not have: privacy and time. He looked round the hall; the ebb and flow of everyday life was going on around them but at that moment they were in some sense isolated from it in this shadowy corner of the great hall. The time was far from perfect, but Max admitted to himself that he couldn't trust himself to endure another night of the torture of sharing a bed with her—knowing that she was so close and yet at the same time so very far away from him, without reaching for her. He might not know much about love, but he did know that breaking down Ionanthe's barriers so that they could share the intimacy of sex without telling her that *he* was Veritas would be unforgivable.

He had to tell her now. He couldn't endure another day of cool silence, during which he was deprived of those small, sometimes silent exchanges of mutual awareness to which he had become accustomed without knowing it until the intimacy was denied him. He had misjudged her, and without meaning to he had also misled her.

When she made to pull away from him a second time, Max bent his head and begged in a low voice, 'Wait. There's something I have to say to you.'

Ionanthe's heart lifted. Hope swelled and rose inside her. He was going to tell her that he loved and needed her more than life itself. He was going to apologise and beg her forgiveness.

She looked over his shoulder. Although the great hall was busy with people, none of them were paying them any particular attention. The hope that he was going to say the words she most longed to hear grew inside her and took wing—only to crash to earth to die painfully when he said, 'You won't like it, I know, but it has to be said.'

The words were enough to send an icy trickle of despair down her spine. She couldn't, she *mustn't* let him see how she really felt.

'If you're going to make more accusations,' she threw back at him, rallying her pride to her defence, 'then I dare say I shan't.'

Max shook his head.

'No, I'm not going to accuse you of anything. The truth is…'

His voice died away as he struggled to find the right words. He was still holding her hand, and now he played with her fingers, stroking them and holding them, his actions such that, had he been a different kind of man, Ionanthe might have thought they betrayed uncertainty. But Max was never uncertain—about anything, she decided bitterly.

'The truth is what?' she pressed him.

'You may remember that you mentioned the Veritas Foundation to me?'

Ionanthe nodded her head, although she couldn't imagine what her praise of Veritas had to do with Max telling her something she wasn't going to like hearing.

'You said how much you admired the…the man who runs it?'

'Yes, I did,' Ionanthe agreed, her eyes darkening with anger. 'You want me to retract what I said because if offends your pride? Is that it?' she guessed.

'No.' Max's voice was terse. His fingers interlaced with her own. 'The truth is—'

'Yes?'

'I should have told you this before, but at the time I didn't think there was any need. It never occurred to me that you'd even *heard* of Veritas, never mind…' He said the words. 'The Veritas Foundation was originally set up by my father. I inherited it from him.'

'*No…*' Ionanthe protested, but somehow she knew that Max was telling her the truth.

'I'm sorry. I never imagined… If I'd known…'

This was so humiliating, so shaming. Hot blood forced its way up under her skin, but she couldn't afford to give way to the chagrin she was feeling. She had made a fool of herself, but Max surely had made even more of a fool of her. Her pride stung, as though it had received a thousand savage cuts.

'You never imagined *what*?' she demanded angrily. 'You never imagined that I might be someone who admired everything I believed Veritas and the man in charge of it stood for?'

Red flags of angry pride might be burning in Ionanthe's face, but because he loved her Max knew that what she was really feeling was pain—the same pain he himself would have felt had their situation been reversed. More than anything he longed to hold her and to take that pain from her.

'I'm sorry.'

'For what? Misjudging me? Destroying my illusions? Believing that I wasn't good enough to know the truth? That I wasn't worthy of sharing your ideals?'

'Ionanthe, don't—please…'

He'd hurt her, and she was justifiably angry. Max understood that, but there was something he still had to tell her. 'I was a fool for not realising that you—'

'No, *I* am the one who was the fool. But not any more, Max,' Ionanthe cut across him bitterly.

Before she could continue Tomas was approaching them, looking self-conscious and uncertain as he addressed himself to Max.

'Highness, the people are asking if you will lead them in the sled race tomorrow, Christmas Eve morning.'

'What sled race is this?' Max asked, looking at Ionanthe. But she shook her head, leaving Tomas to explain whilst her heart sank like a lead weight inside her chest. Her father had led the traditional sled race, and now she wanted to protest in bitter anger that Max should be asked to stand in her father's place.

'It is a tradition of the estate that on the day before Christmas there is a sled race from the top of the ridge behind the castle, and that the race is begun by our lord,' Tomas was explaining eagerly to Max. 'For many years we have not had anyone here to do it, and the old ones are saying that it will bring us luck to have our Prince commence the race for us.'

The people—her people—were showing their approval of Max and their willingness to accept him. Ionanthe felt very alone. Alone and unloved, deceived and misjudged.

Max *had* misjudged her and hurt her, but she had also misjudged him, honesty compelled her to admit. Yes, that was true—but at least he had always known who she was. She hadn't hidden her true self away from him. She hadn't let him talk about his dreams knowing that in comparison to her achievements they were as a child's drawing compared to the work of a master. That was what hurt so badly: knowing that he had excluded her from such an important part of his life; knowing that he had already done all those things she longed so much to do.

Now she could admit to herself what she hadn't really known before. That it was important to her that they met and recognised one another as equals. In her grandfather's eyes she had always been a poor substitute for Eloise. Knowing that, growing up with it, had diminished her. She couldn't allow herself to love a man whose very existence and achievements could not help but do the same.

Their marriage would have to be brought to an end. There was no purpose to it now, after all. Max was the perfect man to rule Fortenegro and to give its people all that they needed. He was also the best role model there could be for his son. Max—the Max she now knew him to be—could achieve far more than she had ever envisaged being able to achieve. There was no purpose in her staying—no need, no role for her, nothing. Ionanthe prayed that fate had been wiser than she had herself, and that she had not yet conceived Max's child.

Max looked towards Ionanthe for guidance as to how he should answer Tomas's request, but her expression was remote and cold. Tomas's interruption had come at the wrong time.

'I shall be pleased to begin the race,' he told Tomas, when Ionanthe continued to ignore his silent request for advice.

The beaming smile with which Tomas received his reply told Max that at least one person was pleased with his response.

She would have to wait until they returned to the palace—until she was sure that she was not carrying Max's child—to inform Max that she wanted their marriage brought to an end, Ionanthe decided. Or maybe she should just leave the island and then tell him. Although of course that would be cowardly. And what if she had conceived? The frantic despairing leap of her heart told her how easy it would be for her to clutch at the excuse to remain married to him.

How Max must have inwardly laughed at her when she had confided to him her admiration for the head of Veritas, unknowingly extolling his virtues, for all the world like some naive teenager filled with hero-worship. All she had to hold on to now was her pride. But she had survived before without love, without anyone to turn to.

That had been different, though. Then she had had hope. Now there was nothing left for her to hope for other than that she did not make even more of a fool of herself than she already had.

Max had married her because his very nature impelled him to want to improve the lot of the islanders. Every move he had made *had* to have been part of a carefully orchestrated plan designed to eliminate what stood in the way of his progress and to move forward with his plans. She couldn't argue with or object to his underlying motivation—after all, she had married him with her own agenda. She couldn't either logically or clinically refuse to understand why he'd had to be so suspicious of her. But pretending to want her—and he *had* done that, even if he had not said the words—allowing her to believe that they shared a mutual desire for one another, that was unforgivable.

And she never would forgive herself for believing even momentarily that he *did* want her. Hadn't she known all along that he had been married to Eloise? Hadn't she known that there were questions she should ask, doubts she should have? But she had wilfully ignored the inner voice that had been trying to protect her.

Whenever she had asked Max about Eloise he had answered that his marriage to her sister had been 'different.'

But it hadn't. He had married them both for exactly the same reason. He had married them because he believed that marriage within their family would help him to gain the acceptance of the islanders and protect their mineral rights. As a person she meant nothing to him. She was simply a means to an end.

CHAPTER FOURTEEN

'So YOU are not going to watch the sled race, then?'
Ariadne kneaded the dough on which she was working
with a fierce pummelling motion that matched the
ferocity of her expression.

'No,' Ionanthe confirmed.

'Hah—I always said that you had your grandfather's
stubborn pride, and look what that got him! So you and
the Prince have had a few sharp words? That's no reason
for you to be sitting here in my kitchen sulking.'

'I know you mean well, Ariadne, but you don't
understand.'

Ariadne gave a cross snort.

'I understand well enough that our good Prince
deserves better than a sulking wife—especially when
anyone can see how much he thinks of you.'

Ionanthe shook her head grimly. 'He married me
because of who I am, Ariadne…'

'Well, I dare say he did. A man would be a fool not
to look about him for a wife who can bring some benefit
to a marriage. But you can't tell me that those soft looks
he keeps giving you when he doesn't think anyone else

is looking don't mean anything, because they do. Look at the way he went out and got you that Christmas tree. It's as plain as plain can be how much he wants to please you, and a man doesn't do that for no reason. I'll tell you now that your father would have had something to say if your mother had behaved like you're doing—showing him up in front of everyone instead of supporting him. I thought our Prince had chosen himself a good wife in you, but now I'm beginning to think I was wrong. You aren't just his wife, and he isn't just your husband. He's our Prince and you are our Princess. That means a lot to folk like us—even if it doesn't to you.'

Ionanthe flinched under the lash of Ariadne's outspoken criticism. The old lady saw things in black and white, but that didn't mean there wasn't an element of truth in what she was saying.

'Quarrel all you want with him in the privacy of your bedroom,' Ariadne continued bluntly. 'There you and him can be just like everyone else. But don't you go forgetting that he's our Prince and you're his wife. The people have expectations of you.'

Ionanthe gave in. 'What is it you're trying to say, Ariadne?'

'I'm saying that your place isn't here in this kitchen, sulking like a child—those days are gone. You should be up on that mountainside, showing yourself as our Princess. It's what the people expect, even if His Highness himself doesn't.'

Ariadne had a point. Her people wouldn't understand why she wasn't there. Her absence would hurt them, and she had neither the wish nor the right to do that.

She looked at her watch, and as though Ariadne had read her mind the cook told her, 'You've still got time. Tomas won't start the race without you being there.'

Ionanthe gave her a grim look, recognising that she had been manipulated and outmanoeuvred.

It was crisp and fresh on the snowy ridge above the steep slope down which the home-made sleds would race. In his teens Max had been a keen winter sportsman, so he was no stranger to the cold and the snow. No stranger to that, but a stranger here nonetheless. An outsider, a man obliged to stand alone, without the woman he loved. Instinctively he looked towards the castle. Only he knew how alone he felt, and how painful that feeling was. How much he wished things were different and he could be free to give all his time and energy to showing Ionanthe how much he loved her.

Ionanthe spotted Max immediately, in a group of men clustered together at the starting point.

'It was lucky I had your father's ski suit stored away,' Ariadne had told Ionanthe earlier. 'The Prince is taller than your father, though.'

Her father's old black racing suit now outlined the breadth of Max's shoulders. Ionanthe knew that there hadn't been a single heart's breath of a second when she had looked at the men from a distance and not known exactly which one he was long before she'd recognised the suit.

She started to walk faster as she climbed the last few yards of the incline.

Those planning to take part in the race had already claimed their sleds from the waiting pile, and the children were watching excitedly as their fathers and elder brothers prepared themselves. The race should have started already, and the children were getting impatient.

One father was smiling at the baby held tight in its mother's arms. An unfamiliar feeling tugged at Ionanthe's heart. The father looked so proud, the mother so lovingly indulgent. It was a matter of great pride and respect to these people that the head of the family showed his bravery and skill on an occasion like this one.

Something made her lift her head and look again to where Max was standing. When she saw he was looking back at her, that he must have been watching her, her heart rolled over inside her chest as fiercely as though it was about to start an avalanche.

She loved him so much.

Her breath made small puffs of white vapour on the cold air as she climbed.

She had almost reached him when a sudden anxious cry went up, and a small boy—no more than five or six years old, Ionanthe guessed, who must have been sitting on his father's sled—suddenly somehow dislodged the sled, which began to rush down the mountainside with him clinging to it.

The course was fast and dangerous, and for that reason the race was forbidden to children. A wave of horror gripped them all for a split second, and then, before anyone else could react, Max dropped down onto his sled and kicked off in pursuit of the little boy.

Ionanthe had watched the race many times, and always admired the skill of the contestants, but never with her heart in her mouth like this, or her partisanship for one man's skill so strong.

Max steered the sled more skilfully than she had ever seen anyone do, Ionanthe acknowledged as she joined in the concerted gasp the onlookers gave as he raced downhill in pursuit of the child. The boy was clinging precariously to his own sled, heading right for the darkly dangerous outcrop of rocks that lay outside the formal lines of the run.

Max would never catch the boy in time, and he too would end up crashing into the rocks. Ionanthe felt sick with dread for them both. What woman watching the man she loved risk his life in such a fashion would not feel as she did now? Her heart leapt into her throat as somehow Max expertly spun his sled sideways across the snow.

He was going to try to cut off the other sled—put himself between it and the rocks. He would never be able to do it—and if he did then the extra weight of the little boy would take Max crashing right into them, the child's life spared at the cost of his own.

'No!' Her denial was torn from her lungs on an agonised cry, and then, just when she feared the worst, somehow Max managed to intercept the other sled and turn it so that it was running alongside his own.

The rocks were so dreadfully close, and getting closer. Max was reaching for the little boy, pulling him off his sled and into his arms, then rolling off his own sled so that he became a human snowball.

Other men were racing down the hill towards them. Ionanthe wanted not to have to watch, not to have to see Max's beautiful body lying still and unmoving in the snow. But she couldn't *not* look—just as she couldn't stop herself from following the men's headlong flight down the steep slope, falling herself a couple of times, only to pick herself up and then wade knee-deep through the snow in her desperation to get to Max.

Incredibly, when she did get there, when she flung herself down in the snow next to his inert body, Ionanthe realised that she was in fact the first to reach him.

Whilst her tears fell unheeded on his snow-frosted face and eyelashes, the small boy he was still holding wriggled out of his grip, wide-eyed and unbelievably unharmed, to be snatched up in the arms of his father who had reached them within seconds of Ionanthe.

A firm strong hand—Max's hand—grasped Ionanthe's and held it. Max's eyes opened and he smiled at her. The voices of the men gathering round them faded as Ioanthe clung to Max's hand, Max's gaze. She was only able to say tremulously, 'You're alive. I thought…' The weight of what she had thought brought fresh tears.

Max lifted his free hand, the one that wasn't holding hers, and brushed them away, telling her tenderly, 'You mustn't cry. Your teardrops will freeze.'

'I thought you were going to be killed.'

'I couldn't let that happen,' Max told her. 'Not when I hadn't told you or shown you how important you are to me—how much I love you and value you. How much I respect you, and how much I can't bear the thought of my life without you. How much hearing you praise the work of Veritas—work which is so important to me and whose importance I haven't been able to share with anyone since my parents died—blew me away with pride and delight. We haven't known each other very long, Ionanthe, but I can tell you honestly that being with you has been like finding the true heart of my life, its true purpose and its true meaning.'

'Oh, Max…'

As she leaned towards him Max cupped her face and lifted himself up so that he could kiss her.

'No—you mustn't,' Ionanthe protested. 'You could be injured. You mustn't move.'

'I won't move—if you stay with me.' His voice grew strong as he added, 'Stay with me, Ionanthe. Stay with me for the rest of our lives and help me to become worthy of the values and hopes we share.'

There was no time for her to do more than nod her head, because the village doctor had arrived, quickly pronouncing that Max had had a remarkable escape and hadn't broken anything, but that he was likely to be badly bruised.

The father and the grandfather of the child whose life Max had saved had, of course, to shake his hand and thank him, and then all the men were hoisting him up on their shoulders for a triumphant journey back to the castle. Ionanthe joined the women and children following in their footsteps.

Surely there could be no frustration as tormenting as that which kept the one you loved at your side but out of the intimate reach you both craved? Ionanthe thought ruefully, as she and Max played their roles in the great hall at the party around the Christmas tree.

They hadn't even been able to snatch a few precious minutes alone together after their return from the accident, such had been the eager demand of her people to thank Max for his bravery.

Now the youngest children were snuggling sleepily in the arms of mothers and fathers as the final carol came to an end and the last cup of spiced wine was drunk.

A sweet, sharp thrill of excitement mingled with apprehension zinged through Ionanthe when at last they were free to leave—circumspectly saying their goodnights, and even more circumspectly walking down the long stone corridor together in silence. But what if she had misunderstood Max earlier? What if he had not meant those oh-so-sweet words he had said, which had completely taken away the sting of her earlier pain?

Ionanthe's heart started to beat faster. They had reached their room. Max put his hand on the door handle and looked down at her.

'It's gone midnight. That means that I can give you my gift.'

He'd got her a Christmas present? Ionanthe felt guilty. 'I haven't got anything for you—' she began.

Max shook his head and told her softly, 'Oh, yes, you have.'

They were inside the room, private and shadowed, warmed by the fire in the hearth and even more by their love.

As Max took her in his arms, Ionanthe protested, 'You're going to be so dreadfully bruised and sore.'

'Tomorrow,' Max agreed. 'But not tonight.'

And then he was kissing her, fiercely and hungrily and demandingly, and she was kissing him back with all the sweetness of her love and all the heat of her desire. And nothing, but *nothing* mattered other than that they were together.

Still holding her, Max reached into the inside pocket of his jacket and removed an envelope, which he handed to her.

'What is it?' Ionanthe asked uncertainly. It looked bulky and formal, and for some reason the sight of it had made her heart plummet.

'It's your Christmas present,' Max told her. 'Open it and see.'

Reluctantly Ionanthe detached herself from him and opened the envelope, hesitating a little before she removed the folded sheets of papers inside it.

That it was some kind of legal document she could see immediately, but it took her several minutes and three attempts to read the first page before what exactly it contained could sink in.

I appoint my wife, Ionanthe, to the board of the Veritas Foundation as co-CEO, with powers equal to my own within that role...

There was more—a great deal more legal jargon—but the meaning was plain enough: Max was entrusting to *her* a half share in the operation of his foundation.

'You really trust me that much?' was all Ionanthe could manage to say.

'More,' Max told her truthfully.

He had wanted to show her beyond any doubt how he felt about her in so many different ways, and he could see from her expression that she knew and understood that.

'Oh, Max. I was so hurt that you hadn't told me about Veritas. I felt… I thought I'd have to leave… I love you too much to have been able to go on as things were. But in reality I misjudged you just as much as you did me.'

'We are equally at fault,' Max comforted her, and he drew her back into his arms. 'We both judged one another because of what our experience with others has taught us.'

'You were right to listen to your instinct and to question my reasons,' Ionanthe admitted. 'I did after all have an ulterior motive for marrying you. I can't deny that.'

'An altruistic motive,' Max corrected her tenderly.

'That *is* something we share—our desire to help the people of Fortenegro,' Ionanthe murmured.

'And is it the only desire we share?' Max teased, asking softly, 'You hesitate—but haven't we come far enough to be as honest with one another in words as our hearts and our bodies have already been? Would it help if I were to go first and proclaim my love and my desire for you?'

He was caressing her body as he spoke, stroking his hands over her back, making her want to melt into him.

'I am not a desirable woman—not like Eloise.' That

pain still remained, and with it some insecurity. 'You were married to her and—'

'In name, but never in deed,' Max told her truthfully.

Ionanthe pushed back to look up at him. 'You mean you never—?'

'Never. I couldn't,' Max told her simply. 'A fact about which she taunted me on more than one occasion—although oddly her taunts never had the same effect on me that yours did.'

Ionanthe went slightly pink. 'That was because I wanted to conceive your son.'

'Yes, I know.' Max's voice was mock-stern. 'You wanted to raise a ruler who would be all the things you believed his father was not—whilst *I* very much want to raise daughters who are everything their mother already *is*. Which of us will be first to get their wish, do you suppose?'

When had they moved towards the bed Ionanthe didn't know. She was just glad that they were there, and that Max was reaching out to her with familiar much loved hands to slowly remove her clothes whilst she did the same to him, accompanied by slow, sweet kisses.

'I can think of nothing I want more than for any son I might bear to grow up to match the goodness of his father,' Ionanthe breathed against Max's skin.

'Nothing?' he teased. 'Can't I tempt you to want anything a little more immediate and personal?'

Ionanthe's smile was warm.

'Mmm…' She joined in the game. 'Do you know, I have the *strangest* longing for a fig?' Her breath caught in her throat when she saw the look Max was giving her.

'But,' she told him, holding his gaze, 'what I long for far more is *you*, my dearest love.'

There was no need for any further words. They were locked in one another's arms and the kiss they were exchanging said everything they needed to know.

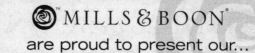

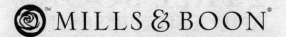

2 FREE BOOKS
AND A SURPRISE GIFT

We would like to take this opportunity to thank you for reading this
Mills & Boon® book by offering you the chance to take TWO more
specially selected books from the Modern™ series absolutely FREE!
We're also making this offer to introduce you to the benefits of the
Mills & Boon® Book Club™—

- **FREE home delivery**
- **FREE gifts and competitions**
- **FREE monthly Newsletter**
- **Exclusive Mills & Boon Book Club offers**
- **Books available before they're in the shops**

Accepting these FREE books and gift places you under no obligation to buy, you may cancel at any time, even after receiving your free
books. Simply complete your details below and return the entire page
to the address below. You don't even need a stamp!

YES Please send me 2 free Modern books and a surprise gift. I
understand that unless you hear from me, I will receive 4 superb new
books every month for just £3.19 each, postage and packing free. I
am under no obligation to purchase any books and may cancel my
subscription at any time. The free books and gift will be mine to keep
in any case.

Ms/Mrs/Miss/Mr_____ Initials _____

_____

Surname _____

Address _____

_____

_____ Postcode _____

Send this whole page to: Mills & Boon Book Club, Free Book Offer,
FREEPOST NAT 10298, Richmond, TW9 1BR